Jacob Abbott

Cousin Lucy among the mountains

Jacob Abbott

Cousin Lucy among the mountains

ISBN/EAN: 9783743339194

Manufactured in Europe, USA, Canada, Australia, Japa

Cover: Foto ©Andreas Hilbeck / pixelio.de

Manufactured and distributed by brebook publishing software
(www.brebook.com)

Jacob Abbott

Cousin Lucy among the mountains

THE
LUCY BOOKS,
BY THE
Author of the Rollo Books.

New York.
Clark, Austin and Smith.

COUSIN LUCY

AMONG THE

MOUNTAINS.

BY THE

AUTHOR OF THE ROLLO BOOKS.

————— ———— ——— ——

A NEW EDITION,

REVISED BY THE AUTHOR

NEW YORK:
CLARK, AUSTIN, MAYNARD & CO.,
3 PARK ROW AND 3 ANN STREET.
1862.

PREFACE.

THIS volume, with its companion, COUSIN LUCY UPON THE SEA-SHORE, is intended as a continuation of Lucy's history, four volumes of which have been already published. They present to the juvenile reader an account of the gradual progress made by our little heroine in the acquisition of knowledge, and in the formation of character, though in very different scenes from those in which the incidents of the preceding volumes have been laid.

1 *

CONTENTS.

CHAPTER VIII.

CHAPTER IX.

CHAPTER X.

CHAPTER XI.

CHAPTER XII.

CHAPTER XIII.

CHAPTER I.

FORDING.

ONE summer afternoon, in the fall of the year, just after sunset, there was a chaise coming down a long hill in the woods. The hill was steep, and there was a rocky precipice on one side of the road. There were lofty mountains all around.

In the chaise there were three persons — a gentleman, a lady, and a little girl. The girl was Rollo's cousin Lucy. The gentleman and lady were her father and mother. They were taking a journey.

The country was very wild and mountainous, and the road desolate and solitary. If it had been morning, Lucy would have been pleased with the cliffs and precipices, and the towering summits of the mountains. But now, as the sun had gone down, it seemed lonely. In fact, Lucy was a little afraid.

"How much farther have we got to go?" she asked.

"I don't know," said her father; "it must be several miles."

"Hark! father," said Lucy, again; "I hear a roaring."

"Yes," said her father; "it is down in the valley below us."

Lucy said nothing in reply to this; but, if her father could have seen her face, he would have perceived that she looked anxious and pale. She did not know what that roaring could be.

"I presume there is a stream there," said her father, — "perhaps a small river."

"O," said Lucy, "a river roaring. I didn't know but that it might be — some — some wild beasts."

Lucy was a little ashamed of her fears, and so she spoke hesitatingly.

Her mother smiled faintly, and then immediately looked serious again. In fact, her mother was a little afraid herself. She did not like crossing rivers so late, in strange and wild places. She was afraid that the bridge might break down.

Lucy's father, however, said that he presumed

that the bridge was perfectly safe, for he thought they would have a good bridge on a road so much travelled as that appeared to be.

He was, however, in error in all his calculations on the subject; for, as it happened, there was no bridge at all. He learned this before he came to the river; for, when they had reached the bottom of the hill, they met a man on horseback, and so they stopped to inquire of him about their road. They asked him if there was a good bridge over that stream; and he said that there was no bridge at all, but that there was a very good place to ford.

"O, I am afraid to ford," said Lucy's mother.

"So am I," said Lucy.

"Is the water deep?" said her father to the man.

"No, sir," replied the man, "not if you keep in the right place, — just in the edge of the rips." So saying, the man rode on.

Lucy's father then moved his horse slowly on down the road, which gradually descended into a ravine, where Lucy could hear the water roaring. Lucy said that she was afraid to have the horse wade through the river.

"So am I,' said her mother

"I don't quite like the adventure myself," said her father, "but there is no other alternative."

"Can't we go back?" said her mother.

"Not very well. It is several miles back to any place where we could spend the night, and then we should have to come and ford this stream to-morrow morning; so that we shouldn't gain much."

"Only it would be light," said Lucy.

"And perhaps we might find some other way," said her mother.

"We'll go down to the bank of the stream, and see, at any rate," said her father. And he accordingly rode on. The rocks and precipices were so high on each side of the road, and the river itself so crooked, winding around among them, that they could not see far before them. At length, however, they came in sight of the surface of the water, gleaming through the trees before them; and in a few minutes more, they came down to the bank of a very broad stream.

"O dear me!" said Lucy; "I am sure I am afraid to wade across such a big river as this."

Her father said nothing, but he stopped the horse upon the sand of the shore, and began to look up and down over the water.

"It looks very shallow," said he.

"What is *shallow*, sir?" said Lucy.

"Why, not deep," replied her father.

"What did the man mean by the *rips*?" asked Lucy's mother.

"He meant the ripples in the water there, all across the stream, just below us." So saying, Lucy's father pointed, and showed Lucy and her mother where the water was rough, being full of little waves, which tumbled along, making a sort of rippling noise. These ripples extended quite across the stream just below where they were. But above them, the surface of the water was calm and smooth, like glass. This calm surface also, like the ripples below, extended across from shore to shore.

The sun had been set for some time, but still there was a great deal of light in the western part of the sky. This light shone upon the water, and enabled them to see, pretty distinctly, the line of the rips, where the man had said that they must go.

"I wouldn't go through the waves, father," said Lucy; "I would go where the water is smooth."

"No," said her father; "we'll follow the directions."

As he said this, he began to drive the horse into

2

the water. The bottom was covered with fine pebble-stones, so that it was by no means as smooth as the road which they had been travelling in: still they got along very well. The water gradually grew deeper and deeper, until it came up to the step of the chaise. They were then in about the middle of the river.

"O father," said Lucy, "what a wide river!"

"Yes," said her father, "it is pretty wide, and I believe I'll stop the horse a minute or two, and let you look about."

So he pulled the reins a little, and said, whoa, and the horse stopped; while Lucy and her mother looked up and down the river. Lucy could see better than her mother, for she was seated in the middle of the chaise, upon a low seat. It was a little farther forward than the seat which her parents were sitting upon, so that she could see up and down the river very well. The reflection of the clouds in the water was very beautiful, and there were trees upon the banks, hanging over into the stream. The river came round between two high hills, a short distance above where they were, and there were crags, and precipices, and high mountains, all around.

"I see one house," said Lucy's mother.

"Where is it, mother?" said Lucy

Her mother pointed towards the house. It seemed to be pretty far off on one side of the valley, far above where they were. They could not see its situation very distinctly, because it was so nearly dark; but it appeared to be on an elevated table of land, with high mountains beyond it.

"There are three houses there," said Lucy "I can see three."

"No," replied her father; "those are the barns, I presume; however, we must drive on."

He accordingly drove on. Lucy watched the house as long as she could. It was not very large, and was painted white, and there was an enormous elm hanging over it, like an umbrella. The barns, which Lucy thought, at first, were other houses, were very large; but they were partly hidden by trees, so that she could not see them very distinctly. And presently, when the horse drew near the shore, the tops of some large pine-trees, which grew upon the bank, came in the way, and they lost sight of the house altogether. When the horse reached the opposite bank of the river, he walked up the ascent, and then came to a smooth and pleasant road, through a level mowing field, with groves of trees upon one side along the bank of the river. The level field did not extend very

2 *

far; and when they came to the end of it, they began to ascend a hill. A short distance before them, they saw a man coming with a cart and oxen.

"I believe I'll stop," said Lucy's father, "and ask him how far it is to the next tavern."

"Yes," said Lucy; "I would."

And just before they met the man, her mother said, in a lower tone, "Ask him, too, whether we shall have to ford another stream."

Just at that minute, they saw that the man was driving his team out of the road, in order to make room for them to pass; for the road here was quite narrow. When they got opposite to him, he stood among the bushes, with one arm resting upon the yoke of his oxen, waiting for them to pass. He nodded to them, with a frank and pleasant expression of countenance.

"Will you tell me, sir," said Lucy's father, "how far it is to the next tavern?"

"Why, it's — not far from five miles — equal to ten."

"How so?"

"O, it's right up and down hill all the way."

"It will take us two or three hours to get there, then," said Lucy's father to her mother. Then he turned to the man again, and said, —

"Shall we have any other stream to ford before we get there?"

"No," said the man, "no *other* stream; but you'll have to cross this same one again about four miles from here."

"Ah!" said her father. — "Is it a pretty good place to cross?"

"Yes, very good," said the teamster.

"Better than it is down here, where we just came across?" said Lucy's mother.

"No," said the man, "not *better* than that; we don't call it any thing crossing there, when the water is as low as it is now."

Lucy's mother said no more, and her father was just about driving on, when he reined up his horse again a moment to say, —

"Then there's no place nearer than five miles, where we can put up to-night."

"Why, yes," replied the man, "there's the General's. I presume you could get accommodated up here at the General's."

"How far is it to the General's?"

"O, about a mile and a half," replied the man.

"Does he make a practice of entertaining travellers?" said Lucy's father.

"Why, no," replied the man, "he does not

exactly make a practice of it; but, then, he's very
glad to see them when they come."

"And he makes a regular charge for it, does
he?"

"O yes," said the man; "you needn't be concerned about that; he's very reasonable in his
charges."

"Well, sir, I'm very much obliged to you,"
said Lucy's father; and he immediately began to
whip up his horse, as if he was in a hurry to go
along. At the same time, he turned his face
away from the man towards Lucy, and seemed to
be trying to keep from laughing. Something appeared to amuse him very much; so much, in fact,
that it seemed to be quite difficult for him to keep
sober until he got by the man.

"What are you laughing at, father?" said
Lucy.

Her father did not answer, but only laughed
the more.

"Father," repeated Lucy, earnestly, "what
are you laughing at? I am sure I don't think we
ought to laugh at that man for telling us about
our way."

"No," replied her father; "I was not laughing
at the man, but only at the queer mistake he
made."

" What mistake ? " said Lucy.

" Why, he thought I was afraid that the General would charge too much for entertaining us; whereas all that I was afraid of was, that he would not charge any thing at all."

" What do you mean by *charge*, father ? " said Lucy.

" Making us pay," replied her father.

" Well, what do you want him to make us pay for ? " asked Lucy.

" O, we shall all feel a great deal more at home at his house, if he is going to receive pay for entertaining us. I shouldn't like to go into a farmer's house, and have him get us some supper, and give us beds to sleep in, and then get us some breakfast in the morning, and then not pay him any thing for all that trouble. But the man thought that I was afraid we should have to pay him too much."

Lucy did not understand exactly what her father meant by speaking of a farmer's house; for the house where they were going was a general's house, she thought, and not a farmer's. However, she said no more about it. Her father said that he had forgotten to ask what the General's name was, and her mother said that she thought the General's house must be the one they saw up

among the hills, when they were coming across
the stream.

"Very likely," said her father, in reply; and
there the conversation ceased. They were all
tired, and so they rode on for nearly half an hour
in silence.

The road was generally up hill, though it was
level sometimes for a short distance; and sometimes it even went down a little way, and then
up again. It curved about also, winding along
around rocks and precipices, and sometimes up
narrow ravines. At one place there was a great
tree growing out from the brink of a precipice by
the side of the road, far above them; and the
tree hung over so far, that Lucy was afraid that
it would fall down upon their heads. But her
father said that he thought there was no danger.
They could hear the river roaring through the
valley far below them on one side of the road,
and now and then they got a glimpse of the water, which was bright by the reflection of the sky.

At length they came to ground which seemed
to be more smooth. There began to be a fence
of rails on one side of the road. Presently the
fence stopped, and a wall began. The wall was
made of rough stones piled up in a row. Pretty
soon there was a wall on the other side of the road

too ; and beyond the wall on one side was an orchard, the trees growing among large rocks, which were scattered about the ground. On the other side were broad, level fields, which looked pretty smooth, though Lucy could not see them very well. Her father said that he thought that must be the General's mowing.

As they drove along, they could see that they were passing different fields, having corn and grain growing in them. These fields appeared to be quite large, and the walls seemed to grow better and more substantial the farther they advanced. Lucy's father said he had no idea that there could have been such a place for a farm among those mountains. Lucy, however, said that she did not see any farm, nothing but some fields.

They soon began to draw near the house. They did not see the buildings until they came very near them ; for there were forests and lofty mountains behind them, which looked dark, and so the barns, and sheds, and granaries were concealed. The house, too, did not show itself until they got almost to it. Lucy saw it first by means of a light from one of the windows. She did not see the light very plainly at first, because it shone through some trees which were in the way ; but presently, when they came into full view of it, they saw that it was a very bright light.

"They've got a good fire," said Lucy's mother, "and I'm glad of it, for I feel cold."

"So do I," said Lucy. "I'm glad they've got a good fire."

Just at this time, her father turned his horse up into a large yard, which extended along by the side of the house. There were various out-build ings all around the yard, and the great elm-tree hung over it like a canopy. The elm-tree was very large, and it stood pretty near the house, so that one half of the branches overhung the house, and the other half the yard. Lucy's father drove up pretty near to the door.

CHAPTER II.

THE GENERAL'S.

Just as the chaise stopped in the yard, Lucy saw a boy coming in from the barn towards the house, with a basket in his hand. He ran along towards the chaise, and Lucy's father asked him if the General was at home.

"Yes, sir," said the boy ; "won't you walk in ? I'll hold the horse while you get out."

"No," said Lucy's father ; "we won't get out yet. But will you be good enough to ask him if he will come to the door a moment."

The boy said he would, and he went into the house. Lucy expected to see a man dressed in uniform, with a gun in his hand, or at least a sword ; and also with a feather in his cap, and an epaulet on each shoulder. Instead of this, however, much to her surprise, the boy came out a moment after he had gone in, conducting a plain-looking man, who appeared just like a farmer.

"Is that the General?" said Lucy, whispering to her mother.

"Hush!" said her mother.

The General had a plain, farmer-like look; his countenance, however, was intelligent and expressive. He seemed very glad to see the travellers. He invited them to come in immediately, — even before he heard their story, — and when Lucy's father had told him what their circumstances were, he said, —

"Yes, yes, — I can accommodate you just as well as not. I am very glad to see you."

Then he told the boy to hold the horse's head, while he took Lucy out, and put her down upon a great flat stone before the door. Then her father and mother got out, and the General took off the trunk, which was strapped on behind, and set it down also upon the stone. He also took out the other baggage, and then told the boy to lead the horse off to the barn, and said that he would send out Joseph to help him take care of him. Then they all went into the house.

Just as they were going in at the door, Lucy said, in a very low voice, to her mother, who was leading her by the hand, —

"Mother, I thought that a general was a kind of a soldier."

"Hush! hush! Lucy," said her mother.

Lucy, therefore, said no more, but went in. She found herself in a large room, with a very large fireplace in one side of it. There were a great many strange things,—that is, things strange to Lucy,—all about the room. There was a long wooden seat, with a very high back to it, by the wall, upon one side of the fire. There was a round-faced, happy-looking girl, sitting on this seat, about as big as Joanna. She was knitting. There was, also, a young man sitting by a window; this was Joseph; and he got up and went out when the party came in, in order to go to the barn, and help take care of the horse. The General and his wife put some chairs before the fire, for Lucy and her father and mother to sit down and warm themselves. Lucy sat down with the rest, but she was so much amazed at the strange things before her,—the great hearth, made of monstrous flat stones, the black iron andirons, with the tops turning over in a curl, and the bright, blazing fire,—that she did not think much about warming herself.

Then Lucy began to look about the room. The light shone brightly upon the floor, and under the tables. Under one table there was a large black dog stretched out straight, with his

chin upon his fore paws, and watching Lucy
with the eye that was turned towards her.   And
every time he heard a noise, he would raise his
head, and prick up his ears, and, after listening a
minute, lay it down again.   In a minute or two,
Lucy saw him lift up his head very suddenly,
and look quite wild.   Lucy heard, herself, at the
same moment, a low and distant sound of whis-
tling, which seemed to be out in the yard.   The
dog started up, and ran towards the door, and
stood there a moment, whining for somebody to
open it.   An instant afterwards, a little girl, whom
Lucy had not seen before, came quick, and opened
the door, and let him out.   Then she went back,
and took her seat again upon a cricket in the
corner.   She seemed to be about as old as Lucy;
and Lucy thought to herself, that she wished she
was acquainted with her, and then she would go
and play with her.   "And at any rate," said
she to herself, "I wish I knew what her name
was."

Her name, in fact, was Ellen.   Lucy learned
her name pretty soon; for the General's wife,
who was Ellen's mother, called her, in a few
minutes, to go and show Lucy and her mother
the way to the bedroom.

"Shall I light a candle, mother?" said Ellen.

'" Yes," said her mother.

Lucy then observed that Ellen went to a sort of open cupboard, by the side of the room, where there were a great many dishes and tins in rows, all nice and bright; and she took down an iron candlestick, with a short candle in it, and came and lighted it by the fire. Then she conducted Lucy's mother, and Lucy herself, out through a door in the back side of the room. The door led into a small passage-way; and, from this passage-way, Ellen opened a door which led into a very pleasant little bedroom. There was a bed in the back side of the room, and a little trundle-bed under it, which Lucy supposed was for her. The middle of the floor was covered with a small carpet. The rest of the floor was painted. There were two windows, with white curtains hanging before them, and between the windows a table, covered with a white cloth. Over the table was a looking-glass; and there was a large pincushion hanging under the glass There was also a lightstand in a corner of the room, with a Bible upon it.

Lucy's father came in immediately afterwards, bringing in some of the baggage; and, while he was putting it down, Lucy went and lifted up the curtain of the window to look out.

3*

"O, what a strange-looking place!" said Lucy "I never saw such a strange-looking place. Come and see, mother."

Her mother went to the window to see. Directly before them, under the window, there was a little green yard, with a stone wall running along the back side of it. Beyond the wall, there were trees and bushes; and the land seemed to descend into a little valley, where Lucy thought she could hear a brook tumbling over stones. Beyond the brook there was a vast forest, rising higher and higher up the declivities of the mountains. The mountains were so high, that Lucy had to move away more of the curtain before she could see the summits. They were steep and gray. Lucy could see them very distinctly; for the moon had come up, and was shining upon them. In a place lower down, there was a great, rocky precipice, which projected out from among the trees. Lucy said to herself, that she was glad Royal did not see it; for, if he did, she knew that he would want to be climbing up to the top of it, and she should be afraid that he would fall.

When Lucy went back into the great room again with her mother, she found that there was a round table set out in the middle of the floor, and spread for supper. The girl, who was sitting upon the great seat, beckoned to Lucy to come and sit with her; and Lucy went. She put down her knitting, and took Lucy up in her lap. At first, Lucy was a little afraid; but the girl looked so good-humoredly and pleasantly upon her, that she soon began to feel at her ease.

"What is your name?" said Lucy, looking up into her face.

"Comfort," said the girl.

"Comfort?" repeated Lucy.

"Yes," replied the girl.

"I never heard of such a name as Comfort," said Lucy.

"What is *your* name?" said Comfort.

Lucy told her what her name was, and then Comfort asked her various other questions about their journey; and, at last, Lucy and Comfort became quite well acquainted. In the mean time, Ellen was very busy helping her mother get the supper. There was a round, flat cake set up before the fire, in an iron thing called a *spider*, to bake, and a pie put down in a corner to warm. At length, Lucy looked up to Comfort again, and said, —

"Why don't you help them get supper?"

"O, I don't do the housework," said Com
"fort; "I spin."

"Spin?" repeated Lucy; "how do you spin?"

"With my spinning-wheel," said Comfort.
"There it stands, in the corner."

Lucy looked in the direction where Comfort
pointed, and she saw a very curious-looking machine, with one great wheel, something like one
of the wheels of her father's chaise, only it was
up in the air, on the top of the machine. The
machine had three legs, too, to stand upon.

Lucy looked at it, wondering, when Comfort
asked her if she had never seen a spinning-wheel.

"No," said Lucy.

"And then you never saw any body spin?"

"No," said Lucy.

"You shall see me, then, to-morrow. I shall
spin all day to-morrow."

"I wish you would show me a little to-night,"
said Lucy.

"Well," said Comfort, "I will."

So Comfort put Lucy down, and led her to
the wheel; and then she took up a long, slender
roll of wool, from a pile of such rolls, which was
lying across the forward part of the wheel, and
began to spin. The wheel made a loud, buzzing
noise, which seemed to Lucy to be very extra-

ordinary indeed. Lucy stood before the wheel, with her hands behind her, looking on, with great interest, at the spinning, and wondering what made it buzz.

Presently, Comfort stopped, and led Lucy back to her seat, saying, "To-morrow you shall see me spin more."

"But I am going away to-morrow," said Lucy, "with my father and mother."

Just then, Lucy saw that the supper was ready, and they were putting the chairs around the table. Not long after supper, Lucy's mother took her into the bedroom, to put her to bed. While they were in the bedroom together, Lucy said that she wished her mother would stay there several days.

"No," said her mother; "we must go on to-morrow. But perhaps we shall stop again when we come back."

"When are we coming back?" said Lucy.

"In about a week," replied her mother.

"Well, mother," said Lucy, "why can't you and I stay here, and let father go on alone, and call for us when he comes back?"

"I should like that," said her mother. "I will ask him."

"Well," said Lucy, with an expression of great satisfaction. "Then I can see Comfort spin."

So, after Lucy's mother had put her to bed, and was going out of the room, Lucy called out to her, just as she was shutting the door, —

"You'll be sure and ask father."

"Yes," said her mother.

"And come back and tell me what he says."

"Perhaps so," said her mother. "Good night."

After her mother had gone, Lucy began talking to herself, as follows : —

"I hope we shall stay here ; then I can see Comfort's lamb. Comfort says she's got a lamb. I wish I had a lamb, — or a little spinning-wheel — if a little one would only buzz. This is the way it went : Buzz — buzz — uz — z-z —."

And in a few minutes, Lucy buzzed herself to sleep.

CHAPTER III.

THE INSPECTION.

Lucy's plan, of having her mother and herself remain at the General's while her father went on to finish his journey by himself, was adopted, to her great joy.

Lucy stood under the elm-tree, and saw him drive away, with great satisfaction, the next morning, soon after breakfast.

As soon as her father's chaise was out of sight, at a curve in the road, where some large trees intercepted the view, Lucy turned round to go into the house. Ellen was standing in the door. Her brother, the boy who had held the horse the evening before, was standing pretty near, and, as he turned to go on towards the barn, he said to Ellen, —

"Ellen, is not this inspection day?"

"Yes," said Ellen, after hesitating a moment, "I believe it is."

"Excellent!" said the boy. "We shall have

some cakes. I am going to eat mine on my clearing."

"Inspection?" said Lucy to herself; "I won der what they mean by *inspection*."

But Lucy did not like to ask, though she wanted to know very much. She did not feel enough acquainted even with Ellen, to ask. She thought she would go in and ask her mother.

She found her mother in the little bedroom, arranging it. She had put a table before the window, in a place where it would be pleasant to sit. She had opened her trunk, and had taken out some paper and writing materials, so as to be ready to write a letter. When Lucy came in, she said, —

"Mother, there is going to be an inspection."

"Is there?" said her mother.

Lucy waited a moment; but her mother did not seem to be particularly interested in what she had said, and asked her no questions about it, but went on arranging some books upon the table, just as if there was not going to be any inspection at all. At length, Lucy said, —

"What is an *inspection*, mother?"

"An inspection?" said her mother, looking up, "why, it is a kind of a review."

"A review, mother? I don't know what a *review* is, any better than an *inspection*."

"Why, it is — a —— I don't know how to explain it to you; — it is a sort of a training, where several companies of soldiers come together, and the general looks at them, and examines their guns, and sees them exercise."

"What is it for, mother?" said Lucy.

"Why, to see if every thing is in good order. But is there really going to be an inspection about here, Lucy?"

"Yes, mother, I am sure there is," replied Lucy, speaking very emphatically, and looking very positive, — "I am sure there is, for Robert said there was."

"Is that boy's name Robert?" asked her mother.

"Yes," said Lucy; "and he said there was going to be an inspection. Do you think you shall let me go and see it, mother?"

"Why, that depends," said her mother, "upon when and where it is to be. I can't tell you till you find out something more about it."

"Well," said Lucy, "I'll go and ask Comfort; I am not afraid to ask Comfort."

So Lucy went out in pursuit of Comfort.

Lucy found Comfort at her spinning-wheel.

4

The wheel was in one corner of the kitchen, by a window. It was a great way from the fire, for the room was very large. Lucy was so much interested, for a time, in seeing Comfort spin, that she forgot about the inspection. Comfort talked with her, and explained something about the spinning-wheel, but did not stop her work First she would whirl the wheel around one way very fast for a few minutes, and then she would stop, and then begin to whirl it the other way. Sometimes she would draw out a long thread of the yarn, and then the yarn would all run up on the spindle.

"Why don't you turn your wheel always the same way?" asked Lucy.

"Because," said Comfort, "I have to turn it one way to twist the thread, and then the other to run it on the spindle."

Lucy did not understand the explanation very well, and so she thought she would look on and see how Comfort did it. But she did it so fast that Lucy could not see. So, after she had stood silently for some time, hearing the wheel buzz, she asked Comfort if there was going to be an inspection that day.

"Yes," said Comfort.

"When is it going to be?" asked Lucy.

" Right after dinner," said Comfort.

" How far is it," said Lucy, " from here ? "

" O, not far," said Comfort; " you shall go ; I'll show you."

So Lucy ran back to her mother, and told her that the inspection was going to be right after dinner, and that it was not far, and that Comfort would go and show it to her.

" Well," said her mother, " you may go whenever Comfort goes; but it is very strange that they are going to have an inspection up here. I am sure I don't see where the troops are to come from."

" Well," said Lucy, " I know there is going to be one, because Comfort said so."

Lucy was right. There was going to be an inspection, but it was very different from the kind that she had imagined. For that day, at dinner, Lucy's mother asked the farmer about the inspection, and where it was to be, and he said, " O, we generally begin at the barn, and so go all around."

" Why, what kind of an inspection is it ? " said Lucy's mother.

" Why, it is not a military inspection," said the farmer, laughing. " Did you think it was a military inspection, Lucy ? " he added, turning to Lucy.

"Sir?" said Lucy.

"It is not a military inspection; it is only an inspection of my farm."

"An't there any soldiers?" said Lucy.

"No," said the farmer, "no soldiers. We inspect the barn, and the sheds, and shop, and then we come into the house and inspect the rooms, and closets, and the cellar, to see if every thing is in order. We cannot show you any soldiers."

"My mother said there were going to be some soldiers," said Lucy.

"No," said Lucy's mother. "I said that I supposed they meant an inspection of soldiers. There may be an inspection of any thing."

Lucy was quite disappointed, when she found that it was not to be an inspection of soldiers.

However, she concluded to go and see it, whatever it was; and accordingly, after dinner, she put on her bonnet, and went out to the door with Ellen, and waited there for the rest to come.

In a few minutes, she saw Robert coming from a building between one of the barns and the shed, with a sort of a box in his hand. The box was somewhat similar to a knife-box in form; and, as in a knife-box, there was a handle in the middle, coming up from the bottom of the box, which Robert took hold of, and brought it by.

" What is that, Robert ? " said Lucy.

" This is the tool-box," said Robert.

" What is it for ? " asked Lucy.

" Why, I always carry about a tool-box at the inspection," said Robert. " Because, sometimes father finds something broken, that he can mend at once upon the spot."

By this time he came up to where Lucy was standing, and he put down the box upon the great stone step, so that she could look into it. The box was not very deep, and it was divided off, inside, into several compartments. There was one long compartment upon one side, which ex tended from one end of the box to the other. In this were several tools. There were a hammer and a gimlet ; and, besides, there were several other tools, which Lucy did not know the names of.

Besides this long compartment, there were several small, square divisions, which had nails and screws in them, of different sizes. Lucy said she never saw so many different kinds of nails. While she was looking at them, Robert began to hear the rattling of wheels in the road, and he exclaimed aloud, —

" O, here comes Eben."

Lucy looked to see. A wagon, with a man

4 *

and a small boy in it, stopped opposite to the
house. The boy appeared to be very young —
younger than Lucy. His face was round, and
his cheeks were red and full. He looked very
sober and anxious, for he was afraid that he could
not get out of the wagon, very well. The man
took hold of his arm, and helped him climb down.
Eben looked towards the ground with an anxious
expression of countenance, as if he thought it
was a great way down.

As soon, however, as his little feet touched the
road, his countenance changed very suddenly,
and he began to leap and scamper off towards
the house, with great glee.

" Well, Eben," said Ellen, " and how do they
do at uncle's ? "

" Pretty well," said Eben. " I'm going there
again some day, and am going to stay there a
whole while."

Lucy smiled, and Robert laughed aloud, at
such an unauthorized combination of terms as
Eben's *whole while*. Eben, however, after look
ing at them in wonder a moment, said, —

" You needn't laugh ; I certainly am."

Just then the General came out, and the whole
party proceeded to the barn. The General
looked carefully all around, to see if every thing

was in its place, and in order. From the barn they went into a sort of room in a shed adjoining it, where there were harnesses and chains, and a number of tools of various kinds. The General looked about, and examined them all. There were a parcel of ropes lying in a corner, and the General asked where they came from. Robert said that he found them up in the garret, and had untied all the knots; he was going to have them for his sleds the next winter.

The General said that they ought to be hung up; and he took the hammer and some nails out of Robert's tool-box, and drove up a row of nails, just under a beam about as high as Robert's head. Then all the children took up the pieces of ropes, and hung them up, one piece on each nail.

" There," said the General, " now you can see what you've got. They are out of the way there, and when you want one, you can come and get any length you like."

Every thing else in the harness room was found in good order, and so they went into the shed. There was a wood-pile there, and some of the wood lay near the foot of the pile upon the ground; for this shed had no floor. One of the logs had a wedge sticking into it. The log was cracked open a little, but not very far, and the wedge was driven fast into it.

" How came this left so ? " said the General.

" Why, father," said Robert, " I began to split this log, but I couldn't."

While he was saying this, the General rolled the log over; and he found two other wedges, lying on the ground, under it, half covered in the chips.

" One wedge in the log, and two in the chips, make three signs of a bad woodman," said the General.

" Why, you see, father," said Robert, " that the ring of the beetle kept coming off, and so I couldn't split it."

The General then took an axe, which was standing in its place pretty near where they were, and with a few heavy blows he split the log, and liberated the wedge which had been held in the cleft. Then he told Robert to put the three wedges upon their shelf, and to carry the beetle, with the loose ring, into the shop, and to put it with the tools that were to be mended.

" When is he going to mend it ? " said Lucy.

" The first rainy day," said Ellen ; " he always sends off all the broken things to the shop, and then he mends them some rainy day."

Before Robert got back from the shop, the in-spection party had gone up a back stairway which led into a kind of garret, over the kitchen part of the house. Here there were a great many boxes and trunks, all, however, in good order. There was a large shelf at one end, with a great many herbs in bundles. Then they all went through a narrow door into another garret over the main body of the house; and thence they came down the front stairs. They found that the door at the foot of the stairs would not shut very well; and the General, after looking at it a moment, said that the latch was out of order.

"Yes, sir," said Ellen, "and I wish you would mend it, for it troubles me every time I want to come up stairs."

"Have you got a file among your tools, Robert?" said the General.

"Yes, sir," said Robert; for Robert had come back, before this time, from the shop, and was fol-lowing them with his box of tools.

The General took out the file, and also the hammer. First he filed the iron of the latch a little; then he hammered it a little, and thus very soon put it in good order.

Ellen said that she was very glad.

They then went into all the rooms of the house, except the little bedroom where Lucy's mother was. They opened all the closet doors too, and looked into them, to see if every thing was in order. When they came into the little room where Ellen slept, there was a little chest in it, where she kept her clothes; and she opened the lid, and asked them all to look in and see if her things were not in order.

After they had thus examined the whole house, they went out at the front door, and thence across the yard into the garden. They walked up and down all the alleys, looking at the beds and borders, to see if all was in proper condition.

It was pretty late in the season, and there were not many weeds growing. Ellen and Robert both had some beds in one corner, where they raised corn, and peas, and beans, for seed.

The General told them it was nearly time for them to gather their beans.

When they came out of the garden, Robert asked his father to look at the hinge of the gate, which, he said, was coming off.

There was a narrow piece of board nailed upon the post, and the hinges of the gate were nailed to that. By some means or other, however, this board had got split where the upper hinge was fastened to it, and so the hinge was loose. Robert pointed it out to his father.

" Ah, yes," said he; " I am glad you showed me this ; very soon the hinge would have come off, and then the lower hinge would have got broken. Now we shall save them."

The General then looked at the board, and said it was split, and there must be a new one made. So he took out some tools from Robert's box, and took off the hinges very carefully. Then he set the gate up by the fence on one side. Then he took off the split board, and gave it to Eben.

" Can you carry that, Eben, into the shop ? " Eben was a very small boy, but he was very glad to help when he could. He took the board, which was not very heavy, but was about as much as he could well carry, and began lugging it along.

" Now, Robert," said the General, " some time this afternoon, I want you to saw out a piece of board just the size of that, and get it all ready to put on. When it is done, carry it out to the gate, and stand it up there. Also put a tool-box there, and an axe, so that every thing will be ready, and then remind me at supper-time to go and put it on. I can put it on in a moment, if you get every thing ready. — And now the inspection is over."

So saying, the General went away, and Ellen said, —

" Well, Robert, you put your tools away, while I go and get the cakes."

" The cakes ? " said Lucy ; " what cakes ? "

" Why, mother always gives each of us a cake, inspection day, so that we may not forget to remind father of it."

Lucy followed Ellen into the house. She supposed that she would go and ask her mother for the cakes, and Lucy wished that she was going to have one too. But Ellen did not go after her mother. She went directly to a closet. As she was opening the door of the closet, she said, —

" Mother always puts our cakes here, on a particular shelf — three of them, all in a row."

They went into the closet, and there they found the cakes ; only there were four, instead of three.

" Why, here are four," said Ellen ; " mother has made a mistake."

" No," said Lucy ; " one must be for me."

" So it is," said Ellen, " I've no doubt. I'll go and ask mother."

She accordingly went off to ask her mother, and presently came back saying that the fourth was for Lucy. And she accordingly gave her one. It was a round cake, not very thick, but it looked as if it was sweet. Ellen carried the other two out, to give them to Robert and Eben.

Lucy went to show hers to her mother. She found her taking a walk under the trees which · Lucy had seen from out the bedroom window. Lucy took hold of her mother's hand with one of hers, while she held the cake in the other; and so she walked along with her, and told her all about the inspection.

Her mother listened with a good deal of interest; and when she had done, she said that she thought it was an excellent plan to have an inspection.

"Yes, mother, and so do I; and I wish you would have one when we go home."

"I think I will," said her mother.

"Once a month, mother," said Lucy; "it must be once a month. The General has it once a month."

"Yes," said her mother, "I should think that about right. I can inspect your Treasury."

"Yes, mother," said Lucy; "I'll keep it in excellent order.

"Only you couldn't mend the broken things about the house, very well," continued Lucy.

"No," said her mother; "but, then, our inspection would not be just like a farmer's. We should inspect drawers, and closets, and cupboards, and such places. I think it will be an excellent plan."

"And a cake for me and Royal, at the end," said Lucy.

"Is that an essential part of the plan?" asked her mother.

"Essential?" repeated Lucy; "what is *essential?*"

"Why, necessary; that is, is it an indispensable part of the plan that there should be cakes distributed?"

"Why, yes," said Lucy; "that is to make us remind you of it. You see, you would forget when inspection day was coming, unless we reminded you; and so we must have a cake."

On reflection, Lucy's mother concluded that this was, as Lucy represented, a very important part of the plan; and she pretty nearly concluded that, when she returned home, she would adopt the inspection system, for her part of the house, cakes and all.

CHAPTER IV.

A WALK.

THAT evening, after the inspection, Lucy and
her mother went out to take a walk upon a high
hill back of the General's house, to see the prospect. Comfort told them that they could get to
the top of it without going through the grass
at all.

" Why don't you want to go through the grass,
mother?" said Lucy.

" Because there may be some dew upon it,
which might wet our feet," said her mother.
" But are you sure, Comfort," said she, " that we
can get up to the top without getting into the
grass?"

" Yes," said Comfort, " I'm sure; and I'll go,
if you wish, and show you the way."

Lucy's mother liked this plan very much; and
so they set off together, about half an hour before sunset. They followed a cart-road down
into a little valley, and went across the brook;

and then they began to climb up by a narrow
and rocky path among the trees. The path was
very steep, and it was much farther than they
had supposed. In fact, Lucy's mother soon began to be very tired. She was not accustomed
to climb up the hills.

Presently they came to a rocky place under
some cliffs, and Lucy's mother said that she believed that she would not go any farther.

"O mother," said Lucy, "I want to go to the
top very much."

"Very well," said her mother; "you may go
with Comfort, if you wish to, and I will ramble
about here. If you don't find me here when
you come down, you may conclude that I have
gone home."

So she turned off, and began to walk along
under the cliffs, gathering blue-bells and other
flowers that grew among the rocks. Comfort
and Lucy left her, and went on up the steep
path.

"O, what a steep place!" said Lucy.

"This is not very steep," said Comfort.
"There are paths up the mountains much
steeper than this."

"Then I don't see how you get up," said
Lucy.

"O, we climb along," replied Comfort "we step up from one stone to another."

The path was very tortuous; that is, it turned and twisted about a great deal among the rocks and around the points of precipices. It was, in fact, a very wild and desolate-looking place; and pretty soon Lucy began to be afraid. She did not know exactly what she was afraid of, but she began to wish that she had staid down below with her mother.

She was not much accustomed to rocks and mountains, and there was something frightful to her in the ragged precipices, the gloomy thickets, and particularly in a dark ravine, which she could look down into in one place. Besides, she thought that perhaps there might be some bears there.

She did not, however, like to acknowledge to Comfort that she was afraid. So, after they had been walking along a little while, she said, —

"How much farther is it, Comfort?"

"Not a great way. Why, are you tired?"

"Why, no," said Lucy, "not exactly; but I wish my mother had come too."

"So do I," said Comfort; "she would like the prospect, I know. We can see away down to the lower falls."

" How far is that ? " said Lucy.

" O, it is several miles, down the valley."

" Is it as many as seventy miles ? " said Lucy

" No," said Comfort, " not quite seventy."

" Is it a hundred miles, then ? " said Lucy.

" Why, a hundred miles are more than seventy, child."

While Lucy had been talking thus, she had been lagging behind Comfort, and seemed reluctant to advance. They had come to a steep place, where they had to climb up a rocky ascent, which turned, in a spiral manner, around the point of a little precipice. There were bushes and briers on each side, growing out of the crevices of the rocks, and from the little patches of earth. Comfort went up a few steps, and then stopped for Lucy.

" Come, Lucy ; why don't you come ? " said she.

" Why, I think, Comfort," said Lucy, " that we had better not go any farther. I think we had better go back and find my mother."

" O, your mother is safe enough, child."

" But I am afraid she'll get lost," said Lucy.

Comfort laughed at Lucy for being afraid that her mother would get lost.

" She can't get lost," said she.   " She can't go

but a very little way under the cliffs before she comes to the end."

" The end of what ? " said Lucy.

" Why, the end of the level place where she can walk," said Comfort. " After you go out there a little way, the rocks go right down, as steep as the sides of a house."

" Then I'm afraid that she will fall down there," said Lucy.

Comfort told her there was no danger ; but Lucy would not be convinced. The more she argued, the less possibility there seemed to be of making any impression. The truth was, Lucy was not really afraid for her mother, but for herself. And the reason which she offered for wishing to return, was only the ostensible reason, not the real one ; that is, it was a reason that she chose to offer, not the one that she really felt. It is of no use to attempt to reply to reasons that are only ostensible, because they are not the ones that really influence the mind ; and so, even if you show that such reasons are not good ones, the person is not convinced any more than before. If Comfort had known that the real reason why Lucy did not want to go any farther, was, that she was afraid herself, perhaps she would have said something to encourage her, and lead her to

go on.   But while she was only arguing against
Lucy's supposed fears for her mother, she was
doing no good at all; for this was not the true
reason.   When, therefore, we attempt to argue
against people's objections to any thing which we
propose, it is very necessary first to be sure that
the objections which they offer are real objections,
not merely ostensible ones.

Presently Comfort proposed to Lucy that she
should go up a little farther, and she would come
to a place where they could see the house.

" How much farther is it ? " asked Lucy.

" Only up to the top of this rock," said Comfort; " come, I'll help you."

So saying, Comfort came down to where Lucy
was standing, and held out her hand to her.
Lucy was still somewhat reluctant to go; but
Comfort told her that they could see the house
and the yard, and very likely they could see the
people walking about there ; and so Lucy, on the
whole, concluded to go.   Comfort helped her up
from one step to another over the ragged stones,
and presently they reached the top.

Then they went through some bushes a little
way, and came out, a moment afterwards, upon a
sort of shelf of rock, where they had a fine
view.

It was not a very extensive view, for the other rocks and trees, rising on each side, intercepted the prospect, excepting in the direction which was down towards the General's house. The house lay almost beneath their feet; and, as Comfort had said, they could see all the buildings, and the yards, and the garden. Lucy saw a large flock of sheep, too, coming up towards the barn, from a green path behind it.

"There, Lucy," said Comfort, "is not this a pleasant place?"

"Yes," said Lucy, "and there's my mother now, just going into the house."

"So she is," said Comfort; "she has got tired of waiting for us, and has gone in. Now, you can go up to the top of the rock with me, for, you see, she is out of danger."

Lucy looked steadily at her mother, and in a moment she began to call out to her with a loud voice, —

"Mother, look at us."

But just as the words were uttered, her mother opened the door, and went in, and Lucy saw the door close after her. Lucy's attention was next arrested by seeing several cows come along a lane behind the house. Comfort said that they were coming from the pasture. Behind the cows were

Robert and Eben. Lucy could see that Eben had a long switch in his hand, and Robert had an axe over his shoulder.

"There are Robert and Eben," said Lucy, "I verily believe."

"Yes," said Comfort, "they are driving home the cows."

"So they are," replied Lucy; "but Robert has got an axe on his shoulder. What has he been doing with his axe, I wonder?"

"O, I suppose," replied Comfort, "that he has been at work upon his clearing this afternoon; and so, after he had done his work, he went and got the cows."

The road in which the cows were coming, led down through a valley, and it looked like a very pleasant road indeed. Lucy asked Comfort where it led to, and she said it led up to the pasture. Then she asked Comfort what she meant by Robert's clearing; and Comfort told her that Robert was clearing a piece of land somewhere up the road, but that she did not know exactly where it was, or what sort of a place it was.

"I mean to go down and ask Robert where his clearing is," said Lucy.

·" Then you will not go up to the top of the rock with me," said Comfort.

" No," said Lucy, " not this time. We have come high enough for this time. I must go down and find my mother. Perhaps she will want me."

" See," said Comfort, " she has just come to the window of her bedroom."

Lucy looked down in the direction in which Comfort pointed, and she saw her mother just taking a seat at the window. Lucy called to her, and waved her hand at her a great deal, but she could not make her hear. She thought that the reason was, because the cow-bells made such a noise; but Comfort told her that it was much farther than it appeared to be.

Lucy stopped to gather a few flowers around the spot where they were standing, and then she and Comfort descended. Lucy was not at all in a hurry to get home, for her fears of the strange and wild scenery around them were much diminished, when she found that they were going towards home. She kept constantly stopping to gather flowers, and to pick up curious fragments of the rocks; and in one place she found some beautiful red berries, which she wanted to gather and carry down to her mother; but Comfort told her that she believed that they were poisonous.

They remained some time at the cliffs where her mother had stopped, and Lucy found a curious place under the rocks, which she called a *den.* It was a rude fissure under the precipice, and it was large enough for Lucy to get into. She said that, if she should be caught out on the mountains in a shower, she could get into her den, and it would not rain upon her.

When they got home again, as they were passing along by the barn, they saw the cows standing in a little green yard, and Robert was just bringing his milking-stool and a tin pail. He was going to milk the cows. Lucy asked Comfort to let her go in and see him milk, and she told her she might go; only she said that she must be careful not to go too near the cows.

So Comfort went into the house, and Lucy went through a little gate into the yard. Ellen came in just after her, bringing a little milking-stool, and pail too, just as Robert had done.

"Are you going to milk, too, Ellen?" said Lucy.

"Yes," said Ellen; "I milk every night."

So Ellen took her seat near one of the cows, and began milking into her pail very fast.

"Why, how easy it is to milk!" said Lucy "I did not know that it was so easy."

Lucy was mistaken in supposing that it was very easy. It is a general rule, that whatever we see done skilfully appears to be done with ease: and as Ellen was a very good little milkmaid, and the milk came down in fine large streams into the pail, Lucy supposed that it must be very easy.

"I wish you would let me milk a little," said Lucy.

"I don't think you can milk," replied Ellen.

"O, yes, I can," said Lucy; "I do harder things than that."

"But I don't think your hand is strong enough," said Ellen.

Lucy held out her hand, and looked at it, and thought it looked pretty strong.

"And, besides," said Ellen, "have you ever learned to milk?"

"No," said Lucy, "I never had any opportunity."

"Then I'm *sure* you can't milk," said Ellen; "for nobody can milk till they have learned."

"But I wish that you would let me try, and see," said Lucy.

Ellen concluded, on the whole, to let Lucy try; so she rose from the milking-stool, and let Lucy take her place.

6

Lucy tried very hard, but the milk would not come. She was very much surprised.

"Why!" said she. Then she tried again; she tugged away with all her strength. "Why! How do you do it?" said she.

Ellen laughed; and the cow, perceiving that some new and inexperienced hand was at work, and not liking to be experimented upon, began to move. Ellen had just time to catch up the pail, when she walked quietly off, two or three steps, and then stood still.

Lucy was frightened, and jumped up and ran.

Ellen took up her stool by its handle, and followed the cow; and, taking her seat again, went on with her milking. Lucy walked off to Robert, and asked him about his clearing.

She did not, however, have the opportunity to get the information which she wished; for just then her mother, who began to think that it was time for her to come down the hill, came to the door to look for her; and seeing her in the yard among the cows, she called to her to come in. When she got to the door, she asked her mother if she was not willing to have her stay there a little longer and see them milk.

"Is Comfort there?" asked her mother.

"No, mother," said Lucy, "but Ellen is."

"I am afraid you may get hurt," said her mother. "The cows may hook you."

Lucy assured her mother that there was no danger; but her mother thought it best for her not to go there again; and so Lucy did not hear any thing about Robert's clearing until the next morning.

CHAPTER V.

ROBERT'S CLEARING.

In fact, Lucy forgot to ask Robert about his clearing until the next morning, after breakfast, when she was out in the yard, and saw him and Eben preparing to go away.

She asked them where they were going.

"We are going to my clearing," said Robert; "and I wish you'd go too, and be our teamster. Then you shall own part of my lamb."

"Have you got a lamb?" asked Lucy.

"No," replied Robert, "not yet; but I am going to have one. As soon as I have got my clearing done, father is going to give me a sheep and a lamb; and you shall own part of the lamb, if you will go and be my teamster."

"Your teamster?" repeated Lucy.

"Yes," replied Robert; "I am swamper, and Eben is ox, and we want a teamster."

"What shall I have to do?" asked Lucy.

"O, you'll only have to drive Eben, when he is hauling the logs."

" Eben can't haul logs," said Lucy.

" Yes he can," said Robert ; " he's a very good ox ; only we want a teamster."

" Well," said Lucy, " I'll go and ask my mother."

Lucy accordingly went in and asked her mother. Her mother wanted to know how far it was to the clearing; but Lucy could not tell. She then wanted to know how long they were to be gone ; but Lucy could not answer that question either. Finally, her mother said that she might go and ask Comfort if she thought that it would be safe for her to go with the boys, and let her opinion decide the question.

Comfort said there would be no danger if Lucy was careful to keep out of the way of Robert's axe. So they all set off together.

They followed the lane where Lucy had seen the cows come down the evening before, for some distance. It led, in a winding direction, up a val ley, with a brook upon one side of the road.

" What a pretty brook ! " said Lucy.

" Yes," said Robert ; " that is the brook that I am going to float down my logs upon."

" Your logs ? " repeated Lucy.

" Yes," replied Robert, " the logs I get off my clearing. I cut them down, and Eben hauls them to the edge of the brook; and then, when there comes a freshet, we're going to tumble them in, and let them float down to the house."

"And then they'll go by," said Lucy, "and down into the river."

"No," said Robert; "I shall have a boom to stop them."

"What is a *boom?*" asked Lucy.

"A long log of wood across the brook, to stop my logs."

The brook which Robert said was going to float down his lumber, was there a small stream, tumbling over rocks along the valley. Presently, however, they came to a place where the valley widened a little, and there was a level piece of ground on one side of it. On the other side, the land descended steep to the very brink of the brook. The low piece of ground was covered pretty thick with tall alder-bushes, twice as high as a man's head; so that the stems of them, when they were cut down, made pretty large poles. There was one spot, where a considerable number of them had been cut down. In the middle of this spot, there was a pile of branches and tops, heaped up pretty high. There were, also, near the edge of the brook, some piles of the wood wh'ch Robert had got out, and which Eben had hauled to the bank. Robert went into this place, and began at once to cut down one of the tallest bushes.

Lucy watched the blows of his axe, until, at last, the tree began to fall. It would have fallen over upon her, had not Robert called upon her to run away. When it was down, Robert cut off the top and all the branches, and these he put on the heap. Then he cut the long pole in two, in the middle. This made two short poles of it. Then Eben came up with a small chain which he had in his hand, and which he had brought with him, and contrived to hook it around one end of one of the poles, and then began to draw it off towards the brook.

" Is that the kind of log you meant, that Eben could draw ? ". asked Lucy.

" Yes," said Robert.

" O, I thought you meant a large log."

" No," said Robert; " we call these our logs. We are going to get a great many piles of them by the brook ; and then, when there comes a freshet, we are coming up here, and going to tumble them in, and let them sail away down home."

Robert cut Lucy a long stick for a goad-stick, and then she drove Eben back and forth several

times, drawing the logs, as Robert called them.
At length, Lucy stopped, and said, —

"But, Robert, what do you mean by *swamper?*
You said that you were swamper."

"Yes," said Robert; "I'm swamper and chopper too."

"I don't understand what you mean by swamper
and chopper," said Lucy.

"Why, when they are cutting trees in the woods,
for timber, they always have a swamper, and a
chopper, and some oxen, and a teamster. The
swamper finds cut which the good trees are, and
he makes a road to them, so that, when they are
cut down, they can haul them out. The chopper
cuts them down, and cuts off the top. Then the
teamster comes with his oxen, and hauls them off
to the river."

"Is that the way?" said Lucy.

"Yes; my father told me," said Robert.

"Why doesn't one man do it all?" said Lucy.

"I don't know exactly," said Robert; "but I
wish I had some fire here, to set my heap on fire."

"Are you going to set that great heap on fire?"
asked Lucy.

"Yes," said Robert, "when I get it big
enough."

"I don't believe it will burn," said Lucy; "it is all green leaves."

"It *will* burn," said Robert, "if I could only get it well on fire. The trouble is, to set it a-going."

So saying, he and Lucy went up to look at the great heap of branches which he had made in the middle of his clearing. Robert said that, if he could find some good dry wood somewhere to begin it with, it would make a noble fire; and he also said that he meant to have brought some fire that morning, but he forgot it. Finally, he said that, if Lucy and Eben would go and get some fire, he would find some good dry wood, and they would have a burning.

Lucy was at first afraid to attempt to bring any fire; but Robert told her that Comfort would give her a lantern, so that it could be brought without any difficulty or danger. Then she was afraid that she should not be able to find her way. But Robert said that Eben knew the way; and so, at last, after much hesitation, Lucy concluded to go. Accordingly, Robert went over, across the brook, to the side of the hill, which was covered with large trees, to see if he could find some old dry log or stump, which he could cut to pieces, and use to kindle his fire. He found one without much difficulty. It was the ruins of an old tree, which the wind had blown over about ten years before. It was leaning against the other trees, and was very much decayed. The limbs had nearly all dropped off, and it looked so dry that Robert thought that, if he could get it down, and split it up, it would be excellent for his fire.

In the mean* time, Lucy and Eben walked along slowly towards the house. When they got there, Lucy sat down upon a chopping-block in the yard, while Eben went in to ask his mother for the lantern. While he was gone, Lucy happened to think that, perhaps, her mother would not like to have her go and help make a fire in the woods, and, at any rate, that she had better go and get leave. She reflected that, if she went without leave, she should feel uncertain and doubtful, all the time, whether she was doing right or wrong; and that would destroy the pleasure of the fire. So she got up, and went into the house to find her mother.

She found her seated at a window in the kitchen, with the General's wife and Ellen, all paring apples for an apple-pudding which they were going to have for dinner.

"O mother," said Lucy, "let me pare some apples."

"O, no, Lucy," said Ellen; "you'll only cut your fingers. It is harder to pare apples, than it is to milk."

The farmer's wife then said that she had better not attempt to pare any apples, but that she might have some to eat; and she gave Lucy two. Just then, Eben came in, out of a back room, with the lantern in his hand. This reminded Lucy of her errand, and so she told her mother what Robert was going to do; and she asked her if she had any objection to her going to see him.

"Why, this is a serious question," said her mother. "I am afraid it would not be quite safe."

"Why, Eben says," replied Lucy, "that they often make fires in the wood, and they never get burnt."

"But you'd be in more danger than Eben," said her mother.

"Why, mother?" asked Lucy.

"Because," said her mother, "in the first place, you are not so accustomed to fires in the woods, and wouldn't know so well where the danger would lie. Besides, your clothes are of cotton, and, if they should take fire, they would burn very fast; but Eben's are woollen."

Lucy looked at her clothes, and at Eben's.

Eben stood by, listening very attentively to what was said, but he made no reply.

" I've a great mind to go with you, and take care of you," said Lucy's mother. " I should like to see the fire myself."

" Well," said Lucy, " that will do. Eben and I will walk on, and you can come after us."

" Very well," replied her mother ; " run along."

Accordingly, Lucy and Eben set off together. Eben had the lantern in his hand, and, after they had gone a few steps, Lucy wanted to look in, and see whether it had not gone out. It was not quite out, but it burned very dimly. Lucy said it was almost out.

" No," said Eben ; " that is the way it always looks."

" Then it isn't a very good lantern," said Lucy.

" Yes, it is a good lantern," said Eben. " It makes a good light in our barn in the winter nights."

" How do you know ? " said Lucy.

" Because," said Eben, " my father carries it out ; and one morning I went out with him, and we found some eggs with it."

" Where did you find them ? " said Lucy.

"O, on a beam. There were four eggs. My father brought in three, and I brought in three."

"O Eben," said Lucy, "that is not right. Three and three don't make four."

"Then perhaps it was ten," said Eben. "Yes, I believe it was ten."

"Why, no, Eben," said Lucy; "it couldn't be ten."

"Why not?" asked Eben.

"Because," said Lucy, "three and three don't make ten."

"What do they make?" said Eben.

. "Why, they make six," replied Lucy. "I'll get a little stick, and make some marks upon the ground, and show you."

So Lucy got a stick, and began making marks upon a smooth place in the road, corresponding with the number of eggs. On more mature reflection, Eben recollected that he brought in two eggs, one in each hand, and that his father carried in two in one hand, and one in the other. He had one egg, he said, in the hand which held the lantern.

"Then there must have been five eggs in all," said Lucy.

In order to prove this to Eben's satisfaction, she made two marks for the eggs which he carried

in, and then two more for those which his father
carried in in one hand, and then, finally, she
added another mark, for the one egg which his
father carried in in his lantern hand.

"Now," said Lucy, "if you'll count them all
up, you'll see that it makes just five, — exactly "

So Eben began to count, —

" One — two — five — six — four."

" O dear me ! " said Lucy ; " why, that isn't
the way to count."

" That's the way *I* count," said Eben.

Lucy looked extremely perplexed, and did not
know what to say ; but just at that moment her
mother came up.   She saw that the lantern
which Eben had put down upon the ground,
while he was listening to his lesson in arithmetic,
was leaning over to one side ; and she was afraid
that the light had got put out.   So she took it up,
and looked into it.

" No," said Lucy, " it has not gone out, but
it burns very dim.   What makes it burn so dim,
mother ? " she asked.

" O, it burns very well.   It looks rather dim,
but that is because it is bright daylight.   A candle
burning in the daylight always looks dim."

Her mother then asked her what she was
making there in the road.   Lucy told her that

"So then began Jasmin" — Page 74.

she had been trying to explain to Eben that two and three made five.

" But," said Lucy, in addition, "I cannot make him understand it. He can't even count."

" Then, of course," replied her mother, " he cannot understand. You are giving him your instructions in the wrong order."

" How, mother?" said Lucy.

" Why, you are trying to teach him addition before he knows how to count. You perceive that a boy who cannot count up to five and six does not know what numbers the words *five* and *six* stand for; and, of course, he cannot tell whether two and three make five, or six, or what they make."

" Then I'll teach him to count," said Lucy.

" Very well," said her mother; " only let us all go along now, for I want to see the fire."

" O, yes," said Lucy; " I forgot all about the fire."

So they all went along together; only Lucy and Eben walked on a little in advance, and Lucy gave Eben some lessons in counting, while her mother followed more slowly, looking for flowers on each side of the way, as she came along.

In a short time, they arrived at Robert's clear-

7 *

ing. They found that he had made fine prepara
tions for the fire. He had cut down the old dead
tree, and chopped it up into short pieces; and
he had pushed these in, under the pile. He also
had some strips of birch bark, which he was going
to kindle with.

Lucy came up to the place with the lantern,
and set it down at Robert's feet. Her mother
came up, too, with a large bouquet of flowers in
one hand.

"That will make a good fire, Robert," said
she; "only it seems to me that you have got the
wood in on the wrong side of the heap.'

"Why?" said Robert.

"Because," replied she, "it ought to be put at
the side towards the wind. Then the wind will
blow the heat and flame directly through the
heap, and set it all on fire. There is not much
wind, but there is enough to do some good."

"We'll try this side first, now I've got it
ready," said Robert.

So he took one of his pieces of birch bark, and,
opening the lantern door very carefully, he put it
in, and lighted it. Now, birch bark, when it is
burning, makes quite a smoke; and Robert put
down this burning piece near the place where he
had put his wood, in order to see which way

the smoke would go. He found that it was drift-
ing off slowly away from the heap of bushes.

" Now, we'll try it on the other side," said he.
He tried to take up his piece of bark, but he
could not. It had curled itself up in a curious
manner, and was all enveloped in flame. So he
took another piece, and lighted it, and carried that
around to the other side of the heap. He put it
in just under the edge of the branches. The
smoke curled up among the branches and leaves,
and they were all very much pleased to observe,
that, instead of sailing off, as it had done on the
other side, away from the heap, it passed directly
through the centre ; and in a few minutes it filled
the whole heap with smoke, which issued out all
over the top of it, as if it was all on fire underneath.

" Yes," said Robert, " I'll move my kindling
wood round to this side."

So he brought his logs round one by one.
They were pretty large, but, being much decayed,
they were not heavy. Robert piled them together in as close and compact a manner as possible ; for he said it was necessary to make a
solid fire.

" Why don't you set the bushes on fire, just
as they are ? " asked Lucy's mother.

" Why, we can't make such brush as this burn
well, alone," said Robert. " It will catch fire a
little, and then go right out, unless we have a
good solid fire underneath it. Then it will all
get to blazing together."

" Let me try," said Lucy, " with a piece of
your birchbark."

" I'll light it for you," said her mother.

So they took a large piece of birch bark, which
Robert handed them, and lighted it in the lantern.
Then they placed it under the heap, at a place
where the sprigs and branches of the bushes
were thickest. The bark soon began to blaze
up well, and immediately the leaves and branches
above it began to take fire.

" There," said Lucy, " it burns."

" Wait," said her mother; " let us see how it
will work."

It blazed up finely very soon, making a bright
flame, nearly a foot high, and the wind blew the
smoke and sparks directly through the top of the
heap. Lucy, and, in fact, her mother, expected
that it would set the whole heap on fire.

Robert and Eben looked on in silence.

In a moment the blaze began to subside. It
burned fainter and fainter, and at last, after a few
minutes, it all died away, leaving nothing but a

hole in that part of the heap, with the bright ends of the twigs, which had been burned off all around, pointing in towards the centre.

By this time, Robert was prepared to put fire to his logs. and he soon got them well on fire. He had pushed them in as far under the heap as he could, and the wind carried the heat and flame through the very heart of it. In a few minutes, large volumes of white smoke came pouring up, out of the top of the pile, in the most beautiful manner. Flashes of flame soon began to break out in the midst of this smoke, and in a short time they all had to stand back from the heat produced by the high, crackling flames. After some time, they all went up upon a bank near by, under some trees, and sat down upon a small log, to watch the progress of the fire.

CHAPTER VI

PHILOSOPHY.

"WHAT a noble great fire!" said Lucy.

"Yes," replied her mother; "in the night I think that that fire would make quite a spectacle."

"Would it burn brighter in the night?" said Lucy.

"No, it would not really burn any brighter, but it would look brighter. It would illuminate the whole sky. It is a fine fire now; but it does not make such a display in the daytime, as it would in the night. Just like the candle in your lantern; you remember how dim it looked. That was because it was surrounded by daylight."

"I should think we could see things better by daylight," said Lucy.

"We can, every thing but fires and lights," replied her mother. "Those we can see better in the night."

"Why is it so, mother?" said Lucy.

"Why, the light of the sun and of the day is so bright that we can't see the light of the fire."

" I don't see why we can't see both, mother,"
said Lucy.

" Why, you see," said Robert, " it dazzles our
eyes, — the light of the sun does, — and we can't
see so well."

" I am sure I can see better in the day than in
the night," said Lucy.

" That's a mistake," said her mother.

" O mother ! " said Lucy.

" In one sense you can ; that is, you can see
more things, because there is so much more light ;
but your eye is not so sensitive."

' What do you mean by *sensitive ?* " asked
Lucy.

" Why, let me see," said her mother ; " how
shall I explain it to you ? "

Here she hesitated, and appeared to be thinking.
Lucy and Robert sat still, and did not interrupt
her. As for Eben, he began to be tired of this
philosophical discussion, and so he got off from
the log, and began to punch a stick down into a
hole under the root of a tree. He thought that it
was a squirrel's hole, and he wanted to make the
squirrel come out.

" Suppose," said Lucy's mother, after a moment's pause, " that I had a small box, tight all
around, excepting at one end, where there was a

small hole, just big enough to look through.   Then
suppose that I should have a picture pasted against
the back side of the box opposite to the hole."

" We couldn't see it, mother," said Lucy ; " it
would be all dark."

" Yes, that's true," said her mother.   " But now
suppose I should make another hole in the side of
the box to let in a little light."

" How could you make it, mother ? " said Lucy.

" O, I don't know, — I could get Royal to bore
it for me with his gimlet."

" That wouldn't be big enough," said Lucy.

" Hasn't he got a big one ? " asked her mother.

" Yes," said Lucy, " he has got one, but it
does not make a good hole ; and then it almost
always splits the wood.   I think it would spoil
the box to have him bore a hole in it with the
large one."

" O," said her mother, " it won't hurt the box ;
it is nothing but an imaginary box."

" An imaginary box ? " repeated Lucy.

" Yes," said her mother ; " it is only an imaginary box, and it won't hurt it to bore an imaginary hole in it."   .

Lucy laughed, and her mother went on with
the illustration

" Now, suppose," said she, " we had such a

box, with a picture pasted on the back part, inside, and a small hole opposite to the picture to look through. Suppose that there was also a hole in the side of the box, to let in a little light. Now, suppose that you were to bring your eye up suddenly to the eye-hole, in the daytime, and also in the night; in which case do you think that you could see the picture most distinctly ?"

"I don't know," said Lucy.

"In the night," said Robert.

"Why ?" asked Lucy's mother.

"Because," said Robert, "I can always see down cellar better in the night than I can in the Jaytime; and that is something like it."

"But I can see down cellar better in the daytime," said Lucy.

"That is because our cellar is lighted with windows," said her mother. "But yours, Robert, is dark, I suppose."

"Yes, ma'am," said Robert; "I never heard of windows in a cellar."

"They sometimes have windows in a cellar," said Lucy's mother, in reply. "But where there are no windows, and you have to take a light down, it is much more difficult to see in the daytime than in the night. So it would be in such a box. If you were to come up to it suddenly in the daytime, you would find that you could see but very little. But if it were possible for you to come to it in the night, and look in, and yet have daylight shine in through the hole in the side, just as before, you would find that you could see much better."

"I'm sure I don't see why," said Lucy.

"The reason is," said her mother, "that a bright light changes the condition of the eye some how or other, — I don't know exactly how, but I know it changes it, — so that it is not so sensitive to light. So, after we have been walking about in the bright day, if we go down cellar with a candle, we can't see very well. Our eyes have been changed in some way by the great light of the day, so that we can't distinguish the objects in the cellar, which are illuminated only by the dim light of the candle."

"If we stay down some time," said Robert, "then we can see better."

"Yes," said Lucy's mother, "because then your eyes become changed again, and adapted to the faint light. They become more sensitive, and then, of course, when you come out again into the bright light of day, they are too sensitive, and you are dazzled."

" Yes, ma'am," said Robert; "that is exactly the way."

Lucy's attention was here taken up by watching Eben, who seemed very much interested in looking into the hole which he had been punching. He was trying whether he could see the squirrel there. She jumped off the log, and went to the hole, saying, —

" Can you see him, Eben?"

" Yes," said Eben, " I believe I can see him."

" Let *me* look," said Lucy.

Lucy put her head pretty close to the hole, and looked very intently.

" Can you see him?" said her mother.

" I don't know," said Lucy, " whether I can see him or not."

" If we had a dark closet here, where we could shut you up a few minutes, then you could see better down in the hole," said her mother.

" Won't it do for me to shut my eyes?" said Lucy.

" I don't know," replied her mother, " whether that will produce the effect, or not. I don't know what it is that causes the eye to change, — whether t is the mere absence of light, or the effort we make to see when looking in the dark. If it were the mere absence of light, then it would answer for you to shut your eyes. You can try it."

The children all tried the plan. They shut their eyes, and held their hands over them, and so kept them as dark as they could for some minutes, and then looked in. They thought that they could see better. Robert said that what Eben saw was only a root, and that he did not believe that there was any squirrel there.

The children, therefore, presently came back, and took their seats upon the log again ; and Lucy asked her mother to go on.

" I think it likely that what I have explained to you may be the reason why a fire or a light does not appear so bright by day as it does by night. The eye is accustomed to the glare, and adapts itself to a strong light, and so becomes in some measure insensible to a comparatively faint one.

" That is the reason, I suppose," she continued, " why we can't see the stars in the daytime."

" Yes, mother," said Lucy ; " I knew there were stars in the daytime. Miss Anne told me."

" I saw a star one morning," said Robert.

" After it was light ? " asked Lucy.

" Yes," replied Robert ; " the sun was almost up."

" I presume it was the morning star," said Lu cy's mother.

" What is the morning star ? " said Lucy.

" Why, you must know," said her mother, " that there is one planet which goes round and round the sun, pretty near to him — a great deal nearer than we are."

" What is a planet, mother ? " said Lucy.

" Why, it is a kind of a world," replied her mother.

" As big as this world ? "

' No; the planet which I was speaking of is not quite so big as this world, I believe ; but it is very large. It goes round and round the sun; and, of course, when the sun rises, and goes over the sky, and sets, this planet keeps with him, going round and round him all the time."

Here Lucy turned her face up to the sky, and began to look for the sun. She put her arm over her eyes, to shade them from the dazzling light.

" O, you can't see it now, Lucy," said her mother.

" Why not ? " said Lucy.

" Because," said Robert, " the sun will dazzle your eyes."

" And besides," said her mother, " the general light makes your eyes less sensitive than they

8 *

ought to be to see a star. We never see this planet by day, although it goes with the sun, sometimes a little before him, and sometimes a little after him, but never a great way off."

" What makes it sometimes before him and sometimes after him ?" asked Lucy.

" Why, that's of course," said Robert.

" No, not exactly of course," said her mother. " It might revolve around the sun in such a way as always to appear to be at the same distance. But, as it happens, it does not. It goes round in such a way that sometimes it appears before the sun, and sometimes behind it, and sometimes it is directly between us and the sun. It passes forward between us and the sun until it gets before him ; then it turns and wheels away around on the other side, and goes on until it gets behind the sun. Then it comes round on this side again ; and so it keeps going and coming.

" But, then," she continued, " we can very seldom see it. There are only three cases in which we can see it. One is, that when it is before the sun, we can see it in the morning ; because, then, you see, it rises first, and so we can see it before it becomes quite light."

" But Robert said it was very light when he saw it," said Lucy.

"Yes, it was much lighter than it had been, but it was not as light as it is at noon."

"No," said Robert; "I only meant it was broad daylight."

"It was much lighter than it was in the night, I have no doubt," said Lucy's mother; "so light, in fact, that you could not see the other stars. But this looks brighter than any other stars."

"Why?" asked Lucy.

"One reason is," replied her mother, "because it is nearer to us; and another reason is, that it is very near the sun, and so is strongly illuminated by his rays."

"But you said that the sun was not up."

"No; but still he was where he could shine on Venus."

"Venus?" repeated Lucy.

"Yes," replied her mother; "that's the name of it. It is very bright. It looks like a little moon when you look at it through a telescope."

"Does it?" said Lucy. "How big does it look?"

"That depends upon the power of the telescope," replied her mother.

"I mean to get up to-morrow morning, and see it," said Lucy.

" You said there were three ways to see it,"
said Robert.

" Yes, mother," said Lucy; " what are the
other two ? "

" Why, sometimes," replied her mother, " Venus falls behind the sun, and then you can't see it
in the morning ; for when the sun rises, Venus is
still down behind the horizon ; and then it does
not come up until after the sun. Consequently,
by the time it gets up, the whole sky is lighted
up, and our eyes are much less sensitive, and so
we can't see it.

" But now," continued she, " if we wait till
evening, the sun, which sets first, will be in advance of Venus, and leave her a little way up
in the sky. To be sure, Venus follows directly
on, and sets in a short time ; but then it generally
gets dark enough before she sets to make our eyes
sensitive enough to see her. When Venus is in
that part of her path which makes her set after
the sun, so that we can see her in the evening,
we call her the *evening* star. When she is
before the sun, so as to be seen in the morning,
she is called the *morning* star. So, you see,
Lucy, it will not do any good to get up early in
the morning to look for Venus, unless we know
whether she is now before or behind the sun.

If she should rise later than the sun, we could not see her."

" Now, there's one more way," said Robert.

" Yes, mother," said Lucy ; " what is that ? "

" Sometimes it happens," said her mother, " that, while Venus, after having been behind the sun, is passing round this side of it to go before it, that it goes exactly between us and the sun, and so we can see it pass across his face."

" How does it look ? " said Lucy.

" It looks like a little black spot," said her mother — " a little, round, black spot, moving across the face of the sun."

" What makes it look so black ? " said Lucy.

" Why, it is only the side which is turned towards the sun that is bright, and the part that is turned towards us, when it passes between us and the sun, will, of course, be dark. Besides," she continued, " I suppose that, strictly speaking, we don't really see Venus in that case at all. We are only prevented from seeing a part of the sun. Venus stops all the rays from that part of the sun which is exactly opposite to her, from coming to us ; and it causes the appearance of a small, round, dark spot, moving along over the face of the sun. That is called a *transit* of Venus. But a transit of Venus happens very seldom."

" I should think it would happen every time Venus comes round," said Robert.

" So should I," said Lucy.

" No," said her mother.

" Because, you see," said Lucy, " that she must go by the sun every time."

" Yes," said her mother; " that is true. But then sometimes she goes above the sun, and sometimes below it. It is very seldom that she goes across, exactly opposite to him ; and it is only then that there is a transit."

" I don't understand," said Robert, " how you can see that little black spot on the sun, when it does go across. I should think the light of the rest of the sun would dazzle your eyes."

" Hark ! what's that ? " said Lucy.

Lucy listened, as if she heard a sound at a distance.

" That's the horn," said Eben.

" Yes," said Robert, " the horn for dinner. We must go home. But first I'll go and put my fire together a little."

The fire had by this time nearly gone down. It had burned out the whole middle of the pile, leaving a circle of brands, ends of sticks, and tops of· bushes, all around. Robert pushed them in to the centre, where they lay upon the burning embers, and soon began to smoke and blaze again. Then he followed Lucy, and her mother, and Eben, who were walking slowly along. When he came up to them, he told them that he knew where there was another heap of brush to burn, and he wished they could come up in the evening, and set it on fire, when they could see the light in all its brightness. This they agreed to do. Then they all went home to try the apple-pudding.

CHAPTER VII.

THE SLAB.

ABOUT an hour after dinner, Lucy and **Eben** went into a shed not far from the barn, where there was a wagon ; and Eben proposed that they should get into it, and play have a ride

" How can we get in ? " said Lucy.

" O, we can climb in," replied Eben.

Lucy thought that she could not climb up into such a high wagon ; but Eben said that it was very easy. So he went around to the front part, and clambered in. Lucy then concluded to try, and she found that she succeeded better than she had expected. She sat down upon the seat of the wagon.

" What a good seat ! " said Lucy. " This is better than a chaise ; for a chaise tips down."

" Tips down ? " said Eben.

" Yes," replied Lucy, " when there is no horse in it."

" What makes it tip down ? " said Eben.

" I don't know," said Lucy ; " but it does, and

I can hardly keep in the seat. But your wagon does not tip down at all."

Just then they heard somebody coming. They looked round, and saw that it was Robert.

"Come, boys and girls," said Robert, "jump out of the wagon."

"Why can't you let us ride?" said Eben.

"Because," said Robert, "I am going to put the horse in."

"Are you going away?" said Eben.

"No, but Comfort is."

"Where is she going?" asked Lucy.

"I don't know," replied Robert; and just as he said so, he opened a door which led out of the shed into the barn, and disappeared. In a few minutes he returned, leading out a horse.

He tied the horse to a ring, which was fastened into a beam about as high as his head, and then went into the harness-room after a harness.

While he was putting the harness upon the horse, Lucy and Eben continued their ride; and presently he told them that they might stay in the wagon, and he would give them a real ride as far as the door. Accordingly, when the horse was harnessed, he backed the wagon out of the shed, while Lucy and Eben sat in it; and then

9

he led the horse up to the door, Lucy holding the
reins, and making believe drive.

Robert fastened the horse to a post, and Lucy
and Eben, thinking that they would not get out
until they were obliged to, sat still. Presently
Comfort came to the door in a different dress
from the one which she had worn when she was
spinning, and with her bonnet on.

" Comfort," said Lucy, " are you going away
in this wagon ? "

" Yes," replied Comfort.

" Who is going to drive you ? " asked Lucy.

" I am going to drive myself," replied Comfort.

" Where are you going ? " said Lucy.

" I'm going a-shopping," said Comfort.

" A-shopping ? " said Lucy ; " I don't see
where you can go a-shopping. Only I wish,"
she added, after pausing a moment, " that my
mother would let me go with you."

" Well," said Comfort, " go and ask her."

Comfort helped Lucy down out of the wagon
and she ran in to ask her mother. As she went
in, Comfort said, —

" Tell her that I should like to have you go
very much."

Lucy came back in a moment, leading her

mother, who came out to see whether it was really true that Comfort was perfectly willing to have Lucy go. When she found that she was willing, her mother consented. At first Eben wanted to go, too ; but Robert persuaded him to go with him. He was going off into the field with a cart, and he said, if Eben would go with him, he would let him ride in the cart. Eben, on the whole, concluded that he would ride in the cart ; and so he got out of the wagon, and went away ; and in a moment after, Comfort and Lucy went riding out of the yard together.

Comfort turned the horse in the opposite direction to the one from which Lucy had come with her father and mother when they first came to the General's. Lucy was glad of this, for she wanted to go in a new road. After riding a short distance along a smooth and level road, they began to descend a hill which seemed to be carrying them down into a dark and shady valley.

The high mountains were all around them ; and now and then Lucy had a view of water down the valley far before them. Lucy thought, too, that she could hear the noise of water tumbling over rocks down in a deep and dark ravine, filled with forests, on the side of the road.

" How far is the place where you are going a-shopping from your father's ? " said Lucy.

" It is about half a mile," replied Comfort.

" O, what a short ride ! " said Lucy. " I'm sorry it isn't farther."

" O, it's farther from here," said Comfort. " It is almost two miles from the General's."

" But I thought the General's was your father's," said Lucy.

" No," replied Comfort ; " my father lives down in the valley, about half a mile from the corner."

" Then why don't you stay there ? " said Lucy. " I should think you would stay at home, and not come and live at the General's."

" O, I come to the General's to spin," replied Comfort.

" I don't see why you come to spin for him."

" Why, he pays me for it," said Comfort.

" O," said Lucy, " then I suppose you spin to get the money."

" Yes," replied Comfort ; " that is it."

" Is your father very poor, then ? " said Lucy.

" No, he is not poor at all.   My father has got a good farm, and is quite forehanded."

" Forehanded ? " repeated Lucy.

" Yes," replied Comfort.

Lucy did not understand what Comfort meant

by *forehanded;* nor did she see why Comfort should go away from home, to live at the General's, to get money, unless her father was poor. However, she was prevented from asking her any more questions by something which here happened to attract her attention.

For just at this time the road descended near to the stream which Lucy had heard in the bottom of the ravine; and there was a large opening through the trees, so that she could see down to the water. It was foaming and tumbling like a cataract, along a very rocky bed. The stream was pretty broad, and there were several rocks and rocky islands scattered about its bed. On one of these islands, at a little distance from the shore, they saw a little boy sitting alone; and he seemed to be crying.

"Only look at that boy," said Comfort. "I wonder how he came there."

So saying, Comfort drew up the reins, and stopped the horse, in the middle of the road. The boy looked up and saw them.

"What's the matter, my boy?" said Comfort, in a loud voice.

The boy answered something, but the roar of the water was so loud that they could not hear what he said.

9 *

"Let's go down and see what's the matter," said Comfort.

"Well," said Lucy, "so we will."

Comfort got out of the wagon, and then she helped Lucy get out. She led the horse to one side of the road, and fastened him. Then she began carefully to descend the bank, helping Lucy down, too. At length they got down to the shore, opposite to where the boy was. He was on the end of a little rocky island, or rather of a large rock, which was out a few steps from the shore. There were scattered rocks about it, and between it and the shore.

"What's the matter, my boy?" said Comfort.

"I can't get off the rocks," said the boy.

The boy did not take any further notice of Comfort and Lucy, than just to answer Comfort's question, but sat still, and continued to cry, just as before.

"How did you get on the rocks?" said Comfort.

"I don't know," said the boy; "I have forgot the place."

"Why, that's very strange," said Comfort, — "such a little boy as this, out on these rocks and saying he don't know how he came there."

"He isn't bigger than Eben," said Lucy.

The water was very shallow in the stream, and there were stones between where the boy was, and the shore, almost near enough for stepping-stones. Comfort looked at them a moment, and then she said, —

"Can't you step over on these stones?"

"No," said the boy, "not unless they come and help me."

"Who come and help you?"

"Why, Roger and the other boy."

"Who is Roger?" said Comfort, "and where is he?"

"I don't know where he is," said the boy.

"He does not know any thing," said Comfort to Lucy, in an under tone. In fact, Comfort was almost out of patience with the boy, because he could not give any better account of himself; though she ought not to have been out of pa tience with him, for he was very small, and then he was very much frightened, both at his situation and on account of the strangers.

"Do you suppose, Lucy, that I could get over on those stones, and help him off?"

"Why, yes," said Lucy, "perhaps so."

"I'm afraid I shall fall into the water," said

Comfort. "Now, if I only had a slab." So saying, Comfort began to look around on the shore.

"A slab?" said Lucy; "what is a slab?"

Lucy had, in fact, never heard of a slab. Comfort did not answer her, for she went immediately away, and began to look about for a slab, Lucy remaining near the boy.

A slab is the outside piece, which is sawed off first, when they saw up a log into boards. Of course, it is round on one side, and flat on the other. Sometimes, too, it is very irregular in shape, on account of the logs not being regular in form. Slabs generally lie in considerable numbers about mills, because they are not of much value; and then, when the freshets come, they get washed away, and carried down the stream. Many of them lodge along the banks, where they get stopped by the trees, or wedged in among the rocks; so that they are often found lying along the shores of such a stream as this was.

By this time, the boy had stopped crying; and he took up a slender little pole, which was lying by his side, and laid it across his lap. Lucy looked at him a moment in silence.

"What is your name, little boy?" said Lucy

"George," said the boy.

"Well, don't be afraid," said Lucy. "Comfort has gone to get a slab."

George did not answer, but he seemed now to be getting quite composed.

"What is that pole for?" said Lucy, again.

"This is my fishing-pole," said the boy.

"Did you come a-fishing?" said Lucy.

"Yes," replied the boy; "and we caught four."

Just at this moment, Lucy heard Comfort calling out that she had found a slab. Lucy looked in the direction from which the voice came, and she saw Comfort beyond a rocky point, a short distance up the stream.

"I've found a slab," said Comfort; "but it is too heavy for me to bring along, and so I'm going to sail it down."

Lucy could see that Comfort was stooping down, as if she was pushing something off the shore. At the same instant, she heard other voices in the opposite direction. She looked down the stream, and saw two boys coming up along the bank, half hid by the bushes and rocks, with fishing-poles in their hands. They were talking together, and did not see Lucy until they got out of the bushes, and had advanced pretty near to her. At the same time, Comfort came down from above, guiding her slab along by a little slender pole.

"O boys!" said Comfort, when she saw them, "is this little fellow your brother?"

"Yes," said one of the boys, "he is my brother."

"We couldn't think how he came here," said Comfort.

"Why, we were fishing," said the boy, "and we wanted to go down and just try a new place; and we told him we'd come back for him in a few minutes, if we found a good place."

"O," said Comfort, "I was just getting this slab, to help him off."

"What did you want the slab for?" said the boy.

"So as to get over where he is," said Comfort.

"O, there's no need of any slab," said the boy. And so, without saying any thing more, he stepped across from one stone to another, as easily as if he had walked along the shore. The other boy followed him, and one of them helped George to the shore, and the other took up a small string of fishes, which was lying in a crevice of the rocks, where Lucy had not seen them.

"You've caught some fishes, then," said Comfort.

"Yes," said the boy; "but they don't bite very well."

"I hope they'll bite better down below," said Comfort; "and I wouldn't leave that little fellow alone again; it frightens him."

"Well, we won't," said Roger.

So saying, the boys all walked along together down the bank, and soon disappeared

"I think he ought to be ashamed of himself," said Lucy. "I would have given him a good scolding."

"That wouldn't have done any good," replied Comfort.

"Yes it would," said Lucy. "It would have taught him not to do so next time."

"No," said Comfort; "that would only have made him more likely to do so again."

"Let's make a bridge with your slab," said Lucy, "and get out on that rock."

"No," said Comfort; "we might get in, and get our feet wet."

"Why, Comfort!" said Lucy; "I don't see that there is any more danger of getting in now, than if the boy was on the rock, and you were going out to get the boy."

"Yes," said Comfort; "but that was an object worth running a little risk for. There's no use in running the risk for nothing ; so, instead of making a bridge of the slab, we'll make a ship of it."

As she said this, she pushed one end of the slab outwards, to make it point out into the stream. It turned slowly, and, when it was pointed in the right direction, she gave it a long push, by which it was sent, by a slow but steady motion, away out into the current. The current immediately turned it down the stream. It went swiftly along the rapids, until presently the end struck against a small rock, which happened to be in its course, projecting a little above the surface of the water. This stopped the force of the motion immediately, and the upper end of the slab began to move slowly round, and to drift sideways down the stream. They watched it a few minutes, and then they climbed up the steep, grassy, and rocky bank, unfastened the horse, got into the wagon, and rode on

CHAPTER VIII.

SHOPPING.

At the place where Comfort and Lucy had found George on the island, the stream looked like a brook, only it was very large for a brook. It ran tumbling along among rocks just like a brook. Lucy found, however, after they had rode along a little farther, that it began to change; and in a short time it appeared to turn into a smooth and beautiful river. This was the sheet of water which Lucy had had an occasional glimpse of, higher up the valley. But now, at a certain turn of the road, they came suddenly upon a full view of it.

"O, what a beautiful river!" said Lucy.

"That's the mill-pond," said Comfort.

"The mill-pond?" repeated Lucy.

"Yes," replied Comfort.

"How did they make such a mill-pond?" asked Lucy.

"Why, they built a dam across the stream,

down below here, and that stops the water, and makes a pond."

"That's an excellent plan," said Lucy. "I think it looks a great deal prettier."

"O, but they didn't do it to make it look prettier," said Comfort.

"What did they do it for?" asked Lucy.

"Why, to make the mills go. They almost always have a pond to make mills go."

"I don't see how a pond can make mills go," said Lucy.

"Why, the dam makes the water rise very high," said Comfort; "and then they build a mill on the bank just below the dam, and have a great wheel down in the bottom of the mill, and they let the water out of the pond against the wheel, and that carries it round so as to make the mill go."

"Do they have a hole in the dam right opposite to the wheel?" asked Lucy.

"Yes, they have an opening," replied Comfort, "and a kind of a long box, to lead the water from the opening in the dam to the wheel. That is what they call the *flume*. I'll show you the flume when we get to the mill."

"Are we going to the mill?" asked Lucy.

" Yes, we shall go over the bridge close to the mill. The flume passes under one end of the bridge."

Comfort and Lucy were now riding along a beautiful road. The mill-pond was on one side, with several islands in the middle, and with many points and promontories extending into the water from the shore, and crowned with trees. On the other side was a great forest, covering the side of a hill, and running higher and higher to the tops of the mountains. On before them Lucy could see a bridge, and a small village on the other side of it. In about ten minutes, they reached the bridge.

Lucy could see the dam very distinctly. It was built of logs laid up like a wall, and extending entirely across the stream, from one side to the other. A thin sheet of water was gliding smoothly over the top, and falling upon the rocks below.

" Why don't they build the dam a little higher," said Lucy, " and so stop all the water ? "

" That wouldn't do any good," said Comfort.

" Yes," said Lucy ; " then they would have more water to make their mills go."

" But they've got water enough," said Com-

fort; " and, besides, if they should make the dam
higher, they could not keep the water from running over the top; because, if they should do it,
it would only stop the water in the pond for a
little while; it would rise higher and higher, and
so, pretty soon, it would run over the top again,
just as it does now."

The mill was on the farther side of the bridge,
and below it, while the dam was above. Lucy
asked where the flume was. Comfort pointed
out to her a sort of a large box or trough, made
of timbers and planks, which proceeded from the
end of the dam on the other side, and passed under the bridge to the mill.

When they got opposite to the flume, Comfort
stopped the horse a moment to let Lucy look
at it. There was a kind of a grating at one end
of it, towards the mill, and the water was whirling
and boiling, among the sticks and slabs which
were lying before the grating. Lucy saw that
the water was running down through the grating,
in underneath the mill, and she supposed it ran
under the water-wheel, and turned it round.

" What makes them throw all those sticks and
slabs into the flume ? " said Lucy.

" They don't throw them in," said Comfort.
" Those things were brought down by the stream,

and came floating along into the flume, and the grating stopped them. That is the reason why they have a grating, — in order to stop all such things."

" Why must they stop them?" said Lucy.

" Because," replied Comfort, " they would go through, and strike against the water-wheel, I suppose, and break it."

After Lucy had looked at the flume long enough, Comfort drove on. The horse ascended a little hill, beyond the brook, and came into a sort of village, though it was very small. It consisted of only a very few houses and shops.

" Where are you going to do your shopping?" asked Lucy.

" I'm going to that store," said Comfort.

So saying, she pointed to a building in a corner, not far from the mill, which was painted green. It had a sign over the door, and some shawls hanging in the window.

" I shouldn't think there was much to buy in that store," said Lucy.

" O, yes," said Comfort; " it is quite a large store."

There were several posts before the store. Comfort drove up to one of them, and got out

10 *

and fastened the horse. Then she helped Lucy out, and they both together went into the store.

It was a much larger and pleasanter store than Lucy had expected. There were two pretty large counters. One was at the back side of the store. There were a great many goods, of all kinds, upon the shelves. At the back corner of the store there was a door, which seemed to open out into a pleasant yard. There were one or two chairs near this door. Comfort conducted Lucy along to this corner, and gave her a seat in one of the chairs.

" Now, Lucy," said she, " I expect it will take me ever so long to do my shopping ; and you may amuse yourself here as well as you can. You can look about the store, or sit here, or go out in the yard."

" Well," said Lucy, " I shall do very well, I don't doubt."

Comfort then went away, and presently came oack with a piece of gingerbread, which she had nought of the storekeeper, and gave it to Lucy. Lucy was glad, both because she liked ginger-oread, and also because she was a little hungry. After she had begun to eat her gingerbread, she tnought she heard a peeping sound out in the yard. Lucy stepped out upon the step to see what it was. She found there, in one corner of the yard, a hen and a whole brood of chickens.

The hen looked rather fiercely at Lucy when she saw that she was coming near her chickens, and so Lucy kept back a little. She observed, however, that the hen had a little leather strap around one of her legs, and by means of that and a string, she was tied to a stake. There was a small cask lying down upon its side, for her to go into, with her chickens.

Lucy broke off a small piece of her ginger-bread, and threw it down to the hen. The hen seized it very eagerly, and broke it into crumbs with her bill, and called her chickens to come and eat it. They all gathered around her, and picked up the little crumbs as fast as they could. Lucy thought that they ate it as if they never had had any gingerbread before.

Lucy looked about the yard. It was a very pleasant yard, descending a little from the street. There was a fence around it painted white; but as the fence was not very high, and as the land descended somewhat towards it, Lucy could see over it. She could see the dam, and the bridge, and the mill-pond, extending far away among the islands and banks covered with trees. She could also look right down the bank opposite to where she stood upon that part of the stream which was below the mill.

She watched the water gliding over the top of the dam, and falling down in a shower upon the rocks below, for a few minutes, when she heard a door open behind her. She looked round, and found that there was another door, besides the one which she had come out of, in the same building. There were also some windows. In fact, it seemed as if the back part of the building was a house, and only the front part a store.

At any rate, the door opened, and a girl, about as big as Lucy, came out with a saucer in her hand, and a spoon in it. Lucy saw at once that she had come out to feed the chickens. Lucy went towards her, to see her; for before she had gone to the front part of the yard to see the prospect.

" Are these your chickens ? " said Lucy.

" Yes," said the girl.

" They're beautiful chickens," said Lucy.

" Yes," said the girl, " only they came too late."

While Lucy was considering what the girl could mean, by saying that her chickens came too late, the girl went on feeding them ; and after she had done, she looked down to the stream which ran off below the mill, and said, —

" Ah! they've shut the gate."

" What gate ? " said Lucy, looking ; " I don't see any gate."

" The water-gate, I mean," said the girl ; — " the gate that lets the water under the mill."

" How do you know that they've shut it ? " said Lucy.

" Because," replied the girl, " don't you see that the water doesn't run under the mill ? When the gate is up, and they are grinding, the water comes tumbling through, under the mill, in a great stream."

Lucy looked, and saw that there was a channel behind the mill, beginning under it, which passed down a little way, and gradually turned, and at length, at a short distance, came out into the main stream. The bottom was rocky, and now nearly bare, only there was a small stream, which ran among the rocks, flowing out towards the main current. There is generally such a channel below a mill, by which the waste water is discharged, after it has performed its duty of giving impulse, in its descent, to the float-boards of the great wheel.

At the place where this channel entered the

main stream, Lucy observed a large, flat surface
of rock, of a blue color, which seemed to be quite
level and smooth. There was a bird upon it,
hopping about. The main current was running
very swiftly along that end of it which was towards the stream, and there was a little water, too,
on each side of it; so that it was a sort of an
island.

"I wish I could go down on that great blue
stone," said Lucy.

"It is very easy to get there," said the girl.
"I've been on it a hundred times."

"I mean to go and ask Comfort to let me go
down and get on it," said Lucy.

So Lucy went into the store, but in a moment
came out again. The girl asked what Comfort
said.

"She says I must not go now," said Lucy,
"but that, when she has done her shopping, she
will go with me."

"Is that the mill-pond up there?" said Lucy,
pointing to the sheet of water above the dam.

"Yes," said the girl.

"What a pretty little island!" said Lucy.

While Lucy was looking at the island, she
happened to observe something upon the water,
very far off, and she did not know what it was.

It looked like a little black line drawn upon the water.

"What is that?" said Lucy, pointing to it.

"What?" said the girl; "I don't see any thing."

"That little black thing, very straight, in the water, close by the island, where that great tree is."

"O, I don't know," said the girl; "nothing but a slab, or something floating down."

Lucy looked at it very intently, and said, —

"I verily believe it is our slab!"

Lucy ran into the store to tell Comfort. Comfort was standing before the counter, looking at some calico. The counter was covered with calicoes.

"Comfort," said Lucy.

"That, you say, is one and ninepence," said Comfort, speaking to the storekeeper.

"Comfort," said Lucy, putting her hand gently on Comfort's arm. "Here's our slab floating down."

"And nine yards, at one and ninepence, comes to how much? — let me see —"

"Comfort," said Lucy.

"Let me see; nine shillings and nine ninepences is — wait a minute, Lucy."

Lucy stood still. The storekeeper drew out

a little slate from under the counter, and began making figures upon it. Lucy saw that Comfort looked perplexed, and was very busy; so she left her, and ran out into the yard again, to watch the slab.

Lucy thought that the slab had not moved at all, while she had been gone. It seemed to be in exactly the place where it was before. In fact, it did not move very fast, because the water in the mill-pond was almost still. It was, however, slowly descending towards the dam.

"Why don't it come faster?" said Lucy.

"Why, the water does not run very fast in the mill-pond," replied the girl; "we can sail all over it in a boat; so that the logs and slabs come down slowly."

"Where will it go to?" asked Lucy.

"O, it will come down over the dam; or else it will run into the flume, and get stopped by the grating."

"I mean to watch it," said Lucy, "and see."

"Then you had better go and stand on the bridge," replied the girl. "You can see it better on the bridge."

"I don't think Comfort would let me," said Lucy.

"You had better go and ask her," said the girl.

"No," said Lucy; "it don't do any good to ask any body any thing when they are a-shopping. They are always talking about ninepence and tenpence."

The girl laughed, and then went into the house.

Lucy looked at the slab a short time, and then, as it did not move much, she got tired of watching it; and so she turned to look at the chickens. She gave them a little more of her gingerbread, and ate the rest. Then she went into the store, and amused herself in walking about, and looking at the things which the storekeeper had to sell.

In about three quarters of an hour from the time when they came into the store, Comfort was ready to go. She had completed her purchases, and the storekeeper had put them all up in one great parcel, with some strong and coarse brown paper wrapped around it. Comfort put her parcel into the wagon, and then told Lucy that she was ready to go.

"Yes," said Lucy, "only you must go down with me to the great blue stone."

"Well," said Comfort, "I will. You've been very patient, and haven't troubled me at all."

So they walked along together towards the bank of the stream below the mill.

11

CHAPTER IX.

AN ESCAPE.

THEY found some difficulty in getting down the bank, it was so steep and rocky. There were, however, little trees and bushes growing here and there, which they could take hold of; and there was a kind of a path, too, which was of considerable service. The channel by which the water came out from under the mill was almost dry, so that they walked about all over it, steping from stone to stone. They went up very near the mill, so that they could see under it. Lucy saw the great wheel, but it was still. She said she wished they would let the water through again, for she wanted to see it go.

"Why, Lucy!" said Comfort; "then the water would come pouring down where we stand. And I don't think that we ought to stay here much longer, for they may hoist the great gate suddenly. So let us go down to your blue stone."

They accordingly walked along over the rocks, towards the blue stone. In the lower part of the bed of the channel, the stones and rocks were wet where they had been covered with water. The higher ones were dry, showing that where the water came through under the mill, they were not covered by it. Comfort told Lucy to step along on the dry rocks, for the wet ones were apt to be slippery.

At length, they reached the great blue stone. Comfort said that it was a beautiful place to stop and see the water. The middle part of the rock was dry ; but it was wet all around the sides, and there was a little water still standing on each side, which they had to step over, in getting upon the rock. There were several chips, and sticks, and small pieces of board on the edges of the rock. They had floated on when the water was high, and had been left there.

Lucy amused herself a few minutes throwing these pieces of wood off into the middle of the current, and seeing them float away down the stream. Comfort took up a long, crooked pole, and pushed off some which were lying in places out of Lucy's reach. After a little while, when Lucy had thrown off all that were upon the front side of the stone, she turned and went to the back side, to find some more. Comfort happened to be standing, at that moment, on the front side

of the stone, reaching out, and trying to push off a
small log which was partly floating, and partly
lodged upon a rock. Just as she succeeded in
pushing off the log, she heard Lucy exclaim, in a
tone of surprise, —

"Why! why! how wide the water is!"

Comfort looked round, and dropped her pole
instantly, and said, —

"So it is; the water is rising. The men have
hoisted the gate. We must get off this rock as
quick as we can."

Comfort and Lucy ran all around the rock,
trying to find a place to get off; but it was too
late. The water, on each side, was before so
wide that they could hardly jump over it, and the
surface of the rocks beyond, which formed the
bed of the stream, sloped off so gradually, that a
very little rise in the water made it considerably
wider.

"What shall we do?" said Comfort; "what
shall we do?" As she said this, she kept going
round and round the rock, trying to find some
place where it would do to jump off; but she
could not. Lucy was very much frightened, and
began to cry.

"O, Lucy, don't cry," said Comfort. "You
needn't be afraid."

"O dear me!" said Lucy; "we shall certainly be drowned."

"O, no" said Comfort; "there's no danger of being drowned. We can stay on this rock, safe, till we contrive some way to get off."

"O, no," said Lucy; "the water keeps rising more and more, and it will cover us all up."

"No," said Comfort; "don't you see that the top of the rock is dry; and that proves it is not covered when the gate is up, and the water runs through as fast as it will."

Comfort looked at the water. It was rising very rapidly; and they could see a torrent of it come pouring down upon them from under the mill, which threatened to raise it much higher. Still Comfort was not afraid. She was confident that it would not come higher than to cover that part of the rock which was wet before, and so that they were safe upon the dry part. And the result was as she had anticipated. The water continued to rise, but it rose more and more slowly; and when it arrived at the old high water mark, — that is, the line where the rock had been wet before,— it continued standing at that level.

"There," said Comfort, "it won't rise any more now."

11 *

Lucy looked very anxious and unhappy. She did not see how they could get off.

"We shall have to stay here all the time," said she, in a very sad and desponding tone.

"No," said Comfort; "there's one way we can do, I'm sure. I can call out to the people in the store, and they'll come and help us off."

"I don't see how they can help us off, if they come," said Lucy.

"O, yes," replied Comfort; "they can go and shut the gate, if they can't do any other way."

"Then that will stop the mill," said Lucy · "and I don't believe they will be willing to stop their mill."

"Yes they will," said Comfort. "I know Mr. Jameson, that owns the mill. He'll stop it for us, I know."

"Well, then," said Lucy, "why don't you call them?"

"Why, I want to look around, and think a little, first," said Comfort. "If we call them, they'll come and help us, I know; but then Mr. Jameson will laugh at me well, and I don't want to be laughed at."

"I had rather be laughed at than be drowned," said Lucy.

"Yes," said Comfort; "but we'll see. I want to look around and think a little. I've heard them say that, if your life is in danger, and you have only got two minutes to save it, you must take one of them to think what to do."

"If we only had a slab," said Comfort, looking around. "And there comes one now, I declare."

Comfort pointed towards the dam. Lucy looked, and behold a slab was just appearing over the edge of the dam. It rubbed along, stopped, then rubbed along again, moving very slowly, as there was scarcely water enough to bring it over. At length, when it had advanced so far that the projecting end was heavier than the other, it fell slowly over, and came down with a thump upon the rocks below. Lucy and Comfort saw all this, for they were standing so low, and the bridge was so high, that they could see the top of the dam under it. As the slab fell down, its face was presented directly towards them; and Lucy said, —

"It is our very old slab, I truly believe. I saw it floating down in the mill-pond, a good while ago."

"I believe it is the very same," said Comfort.

" Now, if I can only reach it with this pole when
it comes by us."

Comfort took up the pole again, and they both
watched the slab, as it came swiftly on towards
the bridge. It struck one of the piers of the
bridge, and then the upper end began slowly to
move round, just as it had done against the stone
where Comfort and Lucy first pushed it off.

"Yes," said Comfort, " it is coming round this
way."

The slab moved slowly, until it got into the
current again, and then it was swept along more
swiftly than ever. It came on towards the side
of the stream where Comfort and Lucy were
standing on the rock ; but Comfort was afraid that
it was not coming quite near enough. She
reached the pole out as far as she could, so as to
have it all ready, saying, —

" Now, Lucy, don't speak a word."

She just succeeded in resting the end of the
pole upon the forward end of the slab.

" There," said Lucy ; " now pull."

But Comfort knew better than to pull. It
would only have pulled her pole off, and let the
slab go down the stream irrecoverably. She
therefore only drew in the pole very gently, but

"Now, Lucy, don't speak a word."— Page 134.

following, at the same time, the natural motion of the slab down the stream. By this means, she succeeded in bringing the slab round into a little sort of bay of still water, below the great blue rock.

"There," said Comfort; "now we'll make a bridge."

Lucy was exceedingly rejoiced to see the slab safe under their control. She was very ready to help Comfort place it. They found some difficulty, however, in doing this, though they succeeded at last. They drew the slab up into the channel on one side of the great stone, where there was a narrow place, and then they pushed the farther end of it up a little way upon the opposite shore. Then they lifted the end which was towards them, and put it upon the rock; and thus they had a bridge.

"Now," said Comfort, "we must go over carefully, for it is slippery. However, there is no danger; for if we get in, it is not very deep, and we shall only get pretty well wet."

But they did not get in. Comfort walked over first very carefully, leading Lucy by the hand, who came behind her. Lucy jumped and capered about upon the bank, when she found that she was free; and they both went up the bank as fast as they could go.

"We got some good by trying to help George off, didn't we?" said Lucy, when they were getting into the wagon.

"Yes," said Comfort.

"It's very lucky, I think," said Lucy, "that we went to get the slab for George."

"No," said Comfort; "it was unlucky, according to the old rule."

"What is the old rule?" asked Lucy.

"Why, that it is unlucky to take pay for doing a kindness."

As they drove down to come upon the bridge, Lucy observed a young man coming along over the bridge, from the other side. Comfort stopped talking, and did not say any thing more until they had passed him. He smiled when he met them, and bowed to Comfort. Comfort nodded to him in return.

"Who was that, Comfort?" said Lucy, when they got by.

"That is Mr. Jameson," said Comfort. "I would not have had him know we got caught down there on the rocks for half a dollar."

CHAPTER X.

EFFECT.

That evening Lucy and her mother set out
to go with Robert to his clearing, to build a fire
for the purpose of seeing how it would look in
the dark. When they were up there in the fore-
noon, Lucy had asked her mother to go up some
evening, as Robert said he had another heap which
he could burn. Lucy wanted very much to see
a fire in the night, and, in fact, her mother did,
too. They asked the General about it at supper-
time, and he said that there was no danger then
in making fires; and so, a little after sundown,
Lucy and her mother set forth, Robert and Eben
coming along close behind them. Lucy carried
the lantern, and Robert his axe.

Lucy had given her mother an account of her
adventure with Comfort on the great stone; and
so strong had been the impression which the affair
had made upon her mind, that she had several
times alluded to it afterwards. And now, as they
were walking along, her mother silently admiring

12

the beauty of the evening, Lucy's thoughts were
away down by the mill,— her imagination being
busy, reproducing images of the great wheel, the
channel below the mill, the wet stones, the slab,
and the current of water.

At last she said, —

"Mother, what makes it unlucky to thank
people for doing a kindness?"

"I didn't know that it was," replied her mother.

"Yes, mother," said Lucy; "Comfort says
it is."

"It seems to me," replied her mother, "that
Comfort is a great authority with you these days."

"I don't know what you mean," said Lucy.

"Why, I think you quote Comfort pretty often."

"Quote her?" repeated Lucy. "I don't know
what you mean: I never heard of quoting any
body."

"What was it she said about its being unlucky?"

"Why, she said it was unlucky to take any
pay for doing a kindness."

"People have a great many sayings," replied
her mother, "about what is lucky and unlucky;
but I haven't much faith in such notions myself."

"I don't see what they say so for, if it is not
true," said Lucy.

"Perhaps they think it is true. Some people think Friday is an unlucky day, and so they never will begin any new undertaking on Friday, if they can help it."

"Do *you* think that it is an unlucky day, mother?" said Lucy.

"No, I don't think it is more unlucky than any other day in the week. It is not a very good day to begin any new undertaking, such as a journey, because it comes so near the end of the week."

"Is that the reason why they call it unlucky," said Lucy, "do you suppose?"

"Perhaps it originated in that. Such notions have generally something or other for a foundation. Though I have heard it said that the reason why Friday has such a bad reputation, is because it was the day of the crucifixion of Christ."

"Did they crucify him Friday?" asked Lucy.

"Yes," replied her mother

"How do they know?" asked Lucy. "It does not say so in the Bible. At least, I never read any thing about Friday in the Bible."

"No," replied her mother; "the account does not mention that particular day ; but it says that he was crucified the day before the Sabbath, and that he rose from the dead the day after the Sabbath."

"Then that would be Saturday," said Lucy "The day before the Sabbath is Saturday."

" Yes, the day before *our* Sabbath is Saturday,' replied her mother; " but the Sabbath in the days of Christ was on Saturday itself; so that the day before was Friday. Jesus was crucified on Friday, and he remained in the tomb over Saturday, which was their Sabbath, and rose from the dead on Sunday morning. So they changed the Sabbath from Saturday to Sunday, in order to have it on the same day that he rose."

" Then that's the reason why they call Friday an unlucky day?" asked Lucy.

" No," replied her mother; " I did not say that that was certainly the reason; only I have heard it said that that might be the reason. There was a time, a great many years ago, when people paid a great deal more attention to particular days than they do now, and celebrated a great many; and perhaps, in those times, they considered Friday, being the day in which such a sad event happened, an unfortunate or unlucky day."

" Well, mother," said Lucy, after a short pause, " but I don't see, after all, why Comfort said it was unlucky to take pay for doing a kindness."

"Perhaps it would tend to make a person act afterwards from mercenary motives," said her mother.

"What does that mean?" said Lucy.

"Why, suppose," said her mother, "that every time you performed any act of kindness for me or your father, I should pay you for it. Then, after a while, when you did any such thing for us, perhaps it would be for the sake of the pay."

"O, no, I shouldn't," said Lucy.

"Well, suppose, then, that Eben is the person. Suppose that you had a great many sugar-plums, and every time he helped you, or did you any kindness, you should give him some of them. Don't you suppose that in a short time, instead of helping you out of feelings of kindness to you, he would do it for the sake of getting the sugar-plums?"

"Why, yes," said Lucy.

"His motive, that is, the thoughts that would lead him to do any thing for you, would be, not honest kindness of heart, but a hope of pay."

"Yes," said Lucy.

"Now, when any person is led by hope of pay to do what he ought to do for other motives, they say he is *mercenary*."

"What does *mercenary* mean?" said Lucy.

"Why, that's what it means," said her mother.
"I've just explained it to you. It is seeking for
pay where we ought not to. Once there was a
lady who was sick, and a boy named Jerry, who
lived pretty near, came to the door, and asked how
she did, and wanted to know if he could do any
thing for her. Now, I suppose you would think
that that was a very kind, generous boy."

"Yes, mother, I should think so," said Lucy.

"He would have been so if his motive had
been as good as it appeared to be. But the fact
was, his motive was mercenary. He had heard
another boy say, that his mother sent him to ask
if he could do any thing for the lady, one day
when she was sick, and that she thanked him, and
gave him a cake. So Jerry thought that, if he
went, perhaps he should get a cake too."

"O," said Lucy, "what a boy!"

"The spirit which he was acting under was
not a benevolent, but a mercenary one."

"Yes," said Lucy, "I thought he really wanted
to know what he could do for the sick lady."

"That was the appearance," replied her mother,
"but it was a false appearance. In fact, appear-
ances, in such cases, are often deceptive. Sometimes, for instance, children go and wish people
a merry Christmas, or a happy new year, when

their motive is, not any real kind feeling, but a hope of getting a present."

Lucy did not say any thing in reply to this. She was silent a moment. She was thinking whether she had not been influenced by mercenary motives, sometimes, in wishing people a happy new year.

" Now, it is very evident," continued her mother, " that when a person takes pay for doing any little act of kindness, that it may tend to make them expect pay in future cases. Now, you happened, in this case, to do George a favor. The consequence was, that, after a time, the benefit of what you did came back to yourselves. This is very apt to be the case with acts of kindness ; and perhaps it is right to tell children so, and let it influence them in some degree ; but still, the real reason, after all, which ought to influence us in doing kindness to others, is simply the good it will do them, and not the hope of having good come out of it, somehow or other, or some time or other, to us."

" Well, mother," said Lucy, " I'm sure that, when we were getting the slab, to help George off, we didn't think of ever getting helped off by it ourselves."

" No, I presume not," said her mother. " But

is it not time for us to get to Robert's clearing? Robert, how much farther is it?" said she, turning round to speak to Robert.

Robert said it was not much farther; and Lucy, who turned round, too, to hear his answer, observed that the light of the lantern flashed upon the trees on each side of the road very beautifully.

"How bright the light shines," said Lucy, "now it is evening!"

"Yes," said her mother, "and if the fire is as bright in proportion, we shall have a splendid illumination."

"O, there's our old fire," said Lucy.

She pointed to the spot where they had made their fire in the morning. It had burned nearly out. There was, however, one little flame coming up from it. The party all gathered around it to see.

"It's the old stump," said Robert.

In fact, Robert had thrown upon the fire, when he went away in the morning, a large, old stump, half decayed, and this had been slowly burning all the afternoon. It was now nearly burnt out · but a piece of the root was blazing up a little. Robert went up to it, and took hold of the part which was not on fire, and then walked off with the burning brand in his hand. He led the way to the other part of his clearing, where he had another heap, and put the brand in under it. He then took the lantern, and went into the woods near by, to find some dry wood to help set the fire to burning. He came back soon, and, in a few minutes, the whole party, standing in a ring around, were illuminated by a bright blaze. A broad column of smoke and sparks ascended into the dark sky, and the bright flashes of light gleamed upon the trees around in a very splendid manner.

"Isn't it a good bright fire?" said Lucy.

"Yes," said her mother; "I want to walk about a little, to see the effect on the trees from different positions."

"The effect, mother?" repeated Lucy.

"Yes; come with me, and I'll show you what I mean by effect."

So Lucy took hold of her mother's hand, and they walked along back to the road. They went up to the top of a little green bank very near the road, and then turned around to look at the fire. It was partly hid by a little group of small trees which intervened; that is, which came between. The fire seemed to be in the middle of these trees. The leaves and branches were brightly illuminated, and in the midst of them they could see the flame

itself glittering through the little openings in the
foliage.   There was a great column of sparks, too,
ascending above the trees and smoke, illuminated
by the fire below.   The sparks were produced by
Robert and Eben, who remained at the fire,
punching it with long poles.

"You see what a beautiful appearance the fire
has here," said Lucy's mother.   "Now, we will
go to some other place, where it will present a different picture, or, as people commonly express it,
where it will have a different *effect*."

So they descended the bank again into the
road, and walked along in it a little way into a
very bright place, where the light from the fire
shone broadly across the road.   When they had
got into the middle of this bright place, they
stopped, and turned towards the fire.   Every thing
in the appearance of it was changed.   The great
glowing flame was full before them.   There was
a sort of circle of trees, around the border of
Robert's clearing, which shone magnificently;
and some rocks across the brook, half under the
trees, seemed to be edged with fire.   They could
see Robert, and Eben too.   Robert was behind
the fire, with his face towards them.   One arm
was extended to push his pole into the fire, and
the other was held up over his face to shade it

from the heat. He looked up to Lucy, and smiled; and Lucy was surprised to observe how distinctly she could see the expression of his countenance and the movement of his eyes, so bright was the illumination. Eben stood on one side *banging* the fire with repeated strokes of his long pole, to make the sparks fly.

"What's that great thing over beyond the brook, mother?" said Lucy.

Lucy pointed to something at some distance across the brook, and beyond some large, scattered trees.

"I don't know," said her mother; "it looks like a great heap of logs and stumps. Let us go and ask Robert."

Robert told them that it was his father's great heap of logs and stumps, that he had got out of a swamp.

"Let's go and set it on fire," said Lucy.

"Will it do to set it on fire?" asked her mother, speaking to Robert.

"It won't burn," said Robert; "it has not been piled up long enough."

"O, we can make it burn," said Lucy.

"Well," said Robert, "we can try."

"Are you sure your father will be willing to have you set it on fire?" said Lucy's mother

"O, yes, ma'am," said Robert, " I know he will ; he wants it burned."

Robert pulled out a large brand from the fire, and gave it to Eben to carry.

" Give me one, too," said Lucy.

" And me," said her mother.

Robert got brands for them all, and they marched along in a fiery procession towards the great heap. They put the brands all together in a hole under the heap, and then went back for more. In this way they soon got quite a little fire burning under the great heap; but still Robert said that he did not believe the heap itself would burn. He said that the logs and stumps were very wet when they were taken out of the swamp, and that they had not had time to dry. The children, however, worked upon it some time, and then left it, and went to the other fire ; and after a while they returned to the great heap again. But they found, as Robert had predicted, it did not appear to burn very well. There was a great smoke coming up out of the middle of it, but they could not decide whether it was going to burn, or whether it was going out. They pushed under some more dry wood, and then waited some time longer. But, at length, Lucy's mother said that it was time to go home, and they

must give up the great heap, and try it some other
time.

Lucy was unwilling to leave it, and wanted to
go and get some more dry wood; but it was hard
work to get it, for the heap was in the middle of
the swampy part of the ground, from where the
materials had been taken, and so they had to
bring the dry wood from some little distance, out
of the woods on the higher land around them.
The ground on which the heap stood was not,
however, wet and swampy then. It was dry and
hard; for Robert's father had dug a drain leading
right through the middle of it down to the brook.

They were, accordingly, obliged to leave the
great heap, though they resolved to come up in
the daytime, when they could get dry wood;
and then, as Robert said, they would keep crowd-
ing dry logs under till they *made* it burn.

CHAPTER XI.

THE GAP AMONG THE MOUNTAINS.

THE next morning, when Lucy got up, the first thing she did, was to go to the window and look out. Her mother was sitting at the table, writing a letter.

" O dear me ! " said Lucy ; " now if the clouds haven't all gone away ! "

" The clouds ? " repeated her mother ; " what clouds ? "

" Why, last evening," replied Lucy, in a desponding tone, " there were some clouds, and a circle round the moon, and Robert said that it was going to rain. And now they have all gone away, and it is going to be pleasant."

" Well," said her mother, " and don't you want it to be pleasant ? "

" No," said Lucy ; " I want it to rain."

" Why, Lucy," said her mother, with surprise, " what do you want it to rain for ? "

" Why, to make a freshet on the brook, to bring

down the logs. And besides, I want my garden to be watered."

"Your garden!" repeated her mother. "I did not know you had any garden."

"Yes," said Lucy; "Ellen gave me one, and my flowers are all dying, because it does not rain on them."

It was true that Lucy had a little garden. It was a small place in Ellen's garden, where Ellen had planted six hills of corn. She had broken off all the ears of corn which had grown there, to roast, and so the stalks which were left were not good for any thing. Ellen, accordingly, pulled them up, and gave them to the cow; and she told Lucy that she might have the place for her garden. So Lucy had hoed it over, and raked it, and put flowers in it, which she and Eben gathered from a field. She had been out the afternoon before, to see her garden, and the flowers were wilted. The reason was, that they had no root; but Lucy thought that it was because they had not been watered by rain.

As the sun rose, it became more and more evident that she was to be disappointed in her wishes for rain. Never was there a finer prospect for a beautiful day. So pleasant was the morning, in fact, that, at breakfast, the General proposed that Lucy's mother should go and take a ride, and see the country around them.

" You and Lucy might take the wagon and Hero," said he, " and have a good ride before dinner."

" Yes," said Comfort; " they might go up through the Gap, and so round by Emery's Pond."

" O, I wouldn't go there," said the General's wife. " It's all rocks and mountains on that road. I think she had better go down to the corner, and out on the Greenville road. There are beautiful farms that way."

" Well, mother," said Lucy, " let's go."

" I don't know as I should be able to manage Hero," said her mother. " I'm not much accustomed to driving."

" No difficulty about that," said the General. " Hero is a good traveller, but you can manage him as easily as you could a dog, with reins or without reins. Or you may take Robert; he'll drive you," continued the General, after a moment's pause. " Robert, couldn't you rig up a seat for yourself in the forward part of the wagon ? "

Robert said he could, without any difficulty;

and finally, after some further discussion, the plan was agreed upon. Robert harnessed Hero, and he put a box in the wagon, in front, for himself to sit upon. They concluded to go around through the Gap; for both Lucy and her mother wanted to see the rocks and the mountains, rather than smooth farms. Just as they were going to set off from the door, the General's wife brought out a tin pail with a cover upon it, and put it into the wagon.

"What is that?" asked Lucy.

"Something for you to eat," said she, "so that, if you like your ride, you can stop and have a little luncheon some where, and so not come back until the middle of the afternoon."

When they drove out of the yard, Robert turned the horse in the direction which led to the fording-place, where Lucy and her father and mother had crossed the stream.

"Why, this is the way we came!" said Lucy.

"Yes," said her mother. "You won't have to cross the ford, shall you?" said she to Robert.

"No, ma'am," said Robert; "we are going to turn off pretty soon."

Accordingly, after they had gone on until they had passed by the smooth fields of the General's farm, they came to a road which turned off to-

13 *

wards the mountains. As they were turning into
this road, Lucy saw a beautiful blue flower, growing under some rocks.

"O mother!" said she, "see what a beautiful
blue flower!"

"Yes," said her mother; "I should like to get
it. We will stop and get it when we come back.
It would wilt and fade away before we get home,
if we take it now."

"But we shall not come back this way," said
Robert, at the same time stopping Hero. "So I
had better get it now."

Robert jumped out, and brought the flower, and
handed it to Lucy. Then he climbed up into
his seat again, and drove on.

"Which way *shall* we come home?" asked
Lucy.

"Why, we are going round by Emery's Pond,
and we shall come out by the Valley district, and
so home by the road that leads by my clearing."

"Where is the Gap that your father spoke of?"
asked Lucy's mother.

"O, it's on here a few miles among the mountains," replied Robert. "This road leads through
the Gap. Father says it would not be possible to
make a road here if it were not for this Gap."

The country grew more and more wild, as they
advanced. The road was very winding, and it
ascended and descended by turns. They were,
however, on the whole, gradually rising, as they
found by observation, every now and then, that they
had a more and more extended view of the great

valley behind them, at the top of each succeeding
ascent to which they attained. It was only occa-
sionally that they had such views, for generally
they were entirely shut in by hills, forests, and
precipices. Before them they saw nothing but
vast piles of mountains, rising higher and higher,
and covered with trees nearly to the summits.
Lucy did not see how they could possibly get
through them or over them. In fact the Gap,
through which they were to pass, was not to be
seen by the traveller until he had entered it.

Once, as they were coming down a little hill,
where the road took a sudden turn, they heard
the voice of a man echoing among the forests
before them.

"What's that?" said Lucy. In fact, Lucy
was a little afraid; and it must be confessed
that the aspect of the whole scene was rather
wild and gloomy.

"That's somebody driving a team," said
Robert.

" How shall we get by?" said Lucy's mother.
" It seems to me the road is very narrow."

" O, we can find a place to get by," said Robert.

Just then, the turn of the road, as they came
down the hill, brought a bridge into view, — a
small bridge, but very high, leading across a brook.
They had passed several similar bridges before,
only this was higher than the others, and looked
more uneven. There were large logs laid along
the edge, on each side of it, for a balustrade

"Why, there's a hole in the bridge," said Lucy's mother.

"Yes, ma'am," said Robert; "there are two or three. But it's no matter. Hero will look out for the holes."

Hero took them over the bridge very carefully, stepping with much deliberation over each hole, or else, where there was room, going entirely on one side of it. Just as they had crossed the bridge, they saw the two heads of a yoke of oxen and a man driving them, coming into view, from a turn in the road, at the top of a little ascent beyond. A large pair of cart wheels followed the oxen. Under the axletree of the wheels was one end of a great log, held up to the axletree by chains. As the team came on, Lucy could see that the other end of the log rested upon the ground, and was dragged along by the oxen.

"Why," said Lucy, "what are they going to do with that great log?"

Her mother looked up to the team with a countenance of great anxiety, for it seemed to be coming directly down upon them. Her fears were, however, in a moment relieved; for the man who was driving the oxen, turned them out to one side of the road, so as to make room for the wagon to go by. One of the great wheels went away down by the side of the road, so that Lucy exclaimed, —

"O dear me! the log will get tipped over."

The teamster, however, did not seem at all

concerned about his log, for he stood leaning against his oxen, and looking at the persons in the wagon, with an expression of great interest and curiosity upon his countenance. He could not think who it was that was coming. He at length nodded slightly to Robert, just as he was going by. He recollected that he had seen him somewhere.

After they had passed, Lucy said to Robert,—

" What is he going to do with that great log? "

" Why, that's Mr. Emery," said Robert ; " he's getting out some boards to cover his house."

There were two things very perplexing to Lucy in this answer. One was, that she did not see any thing like boards. She thought Mr. Emery was getting out a monstrous great log, and not boards. And the other was, she did not know what Robert meant by covering his house.

" Where is Mr. Emery's house," said Lucy.

" O, it's up this way, pretty near his pond," said Robert. " We shall come to it pretty soon."

" Then he's going the wrong way," said Lucy. " He's lost his way."

" No," said Robert, laughing ; " he's hauling that log down to mill, to get it sawed up into boards."

" O," said Lucy, " yes, that's the way he's going to get his boards."

" Yes," said Robert, " that's the way they always get boards."

" That isn't the way my father gets boards,' said Lucy

"How does he get them, then?" asked Robert.

"Why, he buys them."

"I should think he had better get out the logs himself," said Robert, "if he's got any growing on his land."

"My father hasn't got any land," said Lucy, "only just his garden."

"Only his garden?" said Robert.

"No," said Lucy, — "and the yards; nor any oxen."

"Hasn't your father got any oxen, either?" asked Robert.

"No," said Lucy.

"Well," said Robert, "then I don't know what he will do. My father says it's a great deal cheaper to get out the boards yourself, than it is to buy them; but, then, you must have oxen."

By this time, they began to enter the Gap. The mountains and precipices had been growing more lofty, and seemed to draw nearer and nearer to the road, until now they appeared to overhang the valley all around. Sometimes they would pass under a towering cliff of rocks, with trees clinging to the sides, and growing out of the crevices.

From one such precipice Lucy saw water dripping down from a great height, and falling upon some stones by the side of the road.

"O mother," said Lucy, "see the water coming down."

"Yes," said Robert; "that's where the great icicle was last winter."

" Was there a great icicle there ? " asked Lucy.

" Yes," replied Robert, " a monster. 'Twas as tall as the steeple of the meeting-house."

".O, what a big icicle ! " said Lucy. " I should like to see it."

" If you come here next winter," said Robert, " I expect you can see it."

Strictly speaking, it was not an icicle that Robert had seen hanging down on the face of the rocks, the last winter, though it looked like one. It was caused by the freezing of the water, as it dripped down from a vast height. It looked very much like a monstrous icicle clinging to the rock.

Here they came suddenly upon another bridge. Lucy was surprised to see so many bridges.

" How many brooks there are ! " said Lucy.

" O no," said Robert, " only one brook. All the bridges that we have come to, are over one brook. It is the outlet of Emery's Pond."

" What is an *outlet* ? " asked Lucy.

" I don't know," said Robert, " exactly. They always call it the *outlet*."

" What is an *outlet*, mother ? " said Lucy.

" Why, ponds among the mountains," replied her mother, " generally have little streams running into them, coming down from the little valleys, and from springs. And this water must run out again, so that there is generally a place where the water runs out, and that is called the *outlet*."

"And is this brook the outlet to Emery's pond?" asked Lucy.

"Yes,' replied Robert; "and all the bridges which we have come across, are over this same brook."

"What do they have so many for?" asked Lucy.

"Why, they must have a bridge every where, where they want to cross," replied Robert. "The banks are too steep and rocky to ford."

"But why need they cross so many times?" asked Lucy's mother. "Why not keep on one side, or on the other, all the way?"

"Because," said Robert, "they can't make the road. They keep going back and forth across the brook wherever it's easy to make a road. Besides, it is not much work to make a bridge."

"How do they make it?" asked Lucy.

"Why, they cut down a couple of large trees, for *stringers*, — string-pieces, — or else three. I believe they generally have about three."

"What do you mean by *string-pieces*?"

"Why, pieces to go across the stream from one bank to the other, to put the planks on."

"Do they generally have three?" asked Lucy's mother.

"Yes, ma'am," replied Robert, "I believe they do. Then they split up some logs for plank, and so cover it."

"That makes me think," said Lucy, "of what you said about Mr. Emery's house. You said he was going to get some boards to cover it up. What is he going to cover his house up with boards for?"

Robert laughed aloud at this question.

"You needn't laugh," said Lucy. "You said that he was going to cover his house up."

"No," replied Robert. "I said *cover* his house; not cover it *up*."

"Well," said Lucy, "I don't think there's much difference. Besides, I'm pretty sure you said cover it *up*. Didn't he, mother?"

"Let us hear what Robert says he *meant*," replied her mother.

"Why, I meant, *cover* his house," replied Robert; "that is, nail boards on it, to keep out the wind and rain."

"Hasn't he got any boards nailed on his house?" asked Lucy.

"Yes," said Robert, "he's got one room covered in, and he lives in that. He's trying to finish the rest this fall."

It was in vain that Lucy attempted to form a distinct conception of the appearance which Mr. Emery's house would make, with one room covered in, as Robert called it, and the rest waiting for boards yet to be sawed. She said no more, however, but rode on, feeling great curiosity to see the house, and asking Robert to show it to her, as soon as they should come in sight of it.

14

CHAPTER XII.

PUMP–MAKING.

In about a quarter of an hour, they emerged from the Gap, and came out into an open, circular valley, surrounded by lofty mountains. They here crossed the stream again by a log bridge, and rode along afterwards upon its bank; the stream being on their left hand, and woods upon the right.

"Now," said Robert, "we shall soon come to Emery's opening."

"What do you mean by his *opening*?" said Lucy.

"Why, his farm," answered Robert.

While Lucy was considering why they should call a farm an *opening*, she obtained a glimpse of a small sheet of water before them. It was a little pond, shut in among the mountains. They very soon reached it. Lucy saw where the brook came out of the pond. They rode along a little way, by the shore of the pond. On the other side of the road, there was what Lucy called a field of corn and stumps. A little farther on, just in the edge of a group of forest-trees, which remained standing, Lucy saw a small house.

"There's Mr. Emery's house," said Robert.

Lucy looked at the house with great attention.

as they gradually drew near to it. It was small
One end, the nearest end, as they rode towards
it, was covered with boards, which looked new.
The other end was, as Lucy said, all timbers.

" Yes," said Robert; " he hasn't covered but
one room yet. That's what he wants to get
some boards for now, to put on the rest of it."

Lucy saw several small buildings around the
house. They were made of logs and slabs.
There was a large haycock behind the house,
with a roof over it, supported at the corners by
tall poles. In front of the house, there was a
man at work upon a great log. The log was
lying in a horizontal position, each end being
blocked up 'from the ground ; that is, each end
was supported by blocks and logs put underneath.

" What are they doing with that great log ? "
said Lucy's mother.

" I guess they're going to make boards of it,"
said Lucy.

" No," said Robert; " they're boring it. I
expect they are going to make a pump."

" I did not know that they could make a pump
out of a log, ' said Lucy.

" Yes," said Robert; " don't you see he's boring a hole through it ? "

Lucy now observed that the man who was
working at the log, stood at the end of it, and that
he had a tool in his hand, that looked like an
auger. He held the handle of it, and kept con-
tinually turning it round. The iron part entered
into a hole in the end of the log, and Lucy saw

that he was boring a hole into it. She thought,
however, that he certainly could not bore in but a
very little way.

There was a little boy sitting upon the other
end of the log. Lucy could not imagine what he
was doing. She thought that he was too small a
boy to help make a pump; and yet he seemed
to be doing something very busily. As the
wagon drew nearer, Lucy observed that he was
playing horse. He had mounted upon the farther
end of the log, and had tied a string round the
end for a bridle, and was playing that the log
was his horse. He had a stick in his hand,
and was whipping his horse severely, to make
him go.

When the wagon had advanced nearly opposite
to the house, Lucy said, —

"Mother, let us stop a moment, and see the
man make his pump."

"Well," replied her mother, "Robert may
stop a moment, if he pleases."

So Robert stopped his horse opposite to the
end of the log, where the man was at work boring
the hole.

"You've got almost through, John, haven't
you ? " said he.

"Yes," said the young man, "I've only got to
go about a foot farther."

Lucy looked at John, surprised that Robert
should address him so familiarly ; but she observed
that, though he was nearly full grown, and looked
like a man, yet he appeared in his countenance

quite young. She thought it probable that he was one of Mr. Emery's boys, almost grown up. Just at this moment, a woman, very plainly dressed, came out of a back door in the house, with a water-pail in her hand, and walked along a path which led down a descent beyond the house. She looked at the wagon a moment as she went along, but did not stop. Lucy followed the direction of the path with her eye, and she saw that it led down to a little brook not far from the house. There was a log across the brook where the path reached it, and a deep place in the water, just above the log. Lucy saw very plainly that the woman was going to get a pail of water.

Lucy meant to watch her, to see her dip up her water. In fact, she was afraid that she would fall off the log. She was, however, prevented from watching her, by having her attention attracted suddenly to John and his boring; for, just before the woman reached the brook, John began to draw out his auger.

He walked backwards, keeping hold of the handle of the auger with both hands, and drawing it out as he receded. It was a long iron rod, which kept coming out more and more, the farther he went back, till Lucy began to think that the end of it would never come.

" O, what a long borer!" said Lucy.

In fact, the borer was as long as the log. It would do no good to have a log for a pump longer than the auger to be used in boring it; for in that case the hole could not be bored through.

14*

Accordingly, Mr. Emery had cut off his log a little shorter than his auger, in order that it might go through. After John had got the auger out, he did something to the end of it, and then put it in again.

" When are you going to set your pump? " said Robert.

" Father is going to bring up the boxes to-night," said John, " and then we shall set it as soon as we can get it ready."

" Have you got your well dug ? "

" Yes," said John ; " there it is."

So saying, John pointed to a place by the side of the house, where there was a heap of fresh earth, with a hollow place in the middle, and some short boards laid close together in the hollow place.

" We are going to build our barn out beyond there, and so the pump will be handy for the house and the barn too. It is very hard watering the cattle in the brook in the winter, it freezes up so much."

" And, besides," said Lucy's mother, " it is a great way to bring up water to use in the family."

" Yes, ma'am," said John.

Lucy looked down towards the brook, and saw that the woman was coming back, with her pail filled with water. Lucy had just time to see her ; for Robert drove on, and the woman was soon hid behind one of the little buildings. Lucy was, however, very glad to see that she had not fallen in.

" I don't see how he is going to make a pump of that great log," said Lucy.

"Why, when he gets it bored," said Robert, "he will finish off one end of it like a pump, and then they'll let the other end down into their well, and board up close all around it, so that people shall not fall in. Then he'll make a handle."

"I should think it would make rather a rough pump, after all," said Lucy's mother.

"No, ma'am," said Robert; "he'll make a very good pump of it. He's a very good workman."

"I don't see what makes the water come up in a pump," said Lucy.

"The boxes," replied Robert.

"What are the *boxes?*" asked Lucy.

"Why, they're — they're — little things in the pump. Didn't you ever see boxes?"

"Yes," said Lucy, "a great many times." Lucy meant common boxes, not pump-boxes.

"Well," said Robert, "you know the little clapper."

"No," said Lucy; "I don't remember any clappers."

"Why, yes," said Robert, "a little clapper made of leather."

"No," said Lucy; "there is not any clapper in any of the boxes I ever saw."

"Then you never saw any pump-boxes," said Robert.

"Why," said Lucy, "are they different from any other kind of boxes?"

"Yes," exclaimed Robert, emphatically, "altogether different. There is a little leather clapper, that lets the water up, and then keeps it from going down again."

But Lucy could not understand how any thing could be contrived to let the water come up, and then keep it from going down. Robert told her about the upper box and the lower box; but he did not succeed in making it plain to her. In fact, it requires considerable skill in the art of describing and explaining, to communicate any clear idea of the internal construction and working of a pump. Lucy could not get any idea of it whatever. She asked her mother to explain it to her; but her mother said that she did not understand it very well herself. So Lucy said she did not know what she should do.

The road led them, for a time, along the shores of the pond, and generally not much above the water. And, as they passed along, they could see the water on one side of them, and sometimes they had forests, and sometimes steep rocks, on the other. At length, they came to a place where Lucy proposed that they should stop and eat their luncheon. It was a place where a brook flowed into the pond. The road crossed the brook by a bridge, just above its juncture with the pond; so that, when they were on the bridge, they could see the pond below them, between the steep banks of the ravine, through which the brook flowed. One of the banks was an almost perpendicular cliff of rock. The other was not quite so abrupt, and it was covered with trees They could see that down upon the shore of the pond, there was a smooth, sandy beach, extending along the shore on each side of the mouth of the brook. Lucy proposed that they should stop here.

" Well," said her mother, " I think it will be a
very good plan."

" Yes, ma'am," said Robert; " there is plenty
of good grass about here, too, for Hero."

Lucy had not noticed the grass; but now she
observed that, on each side of the road, and near
the banks of the brook, above the bridge, there
was plenty of grass. So they all got out.

Robert began to unharness the horse, after
driving him a little way out of the road. Lucy
stood on the end of the bridge, looking at him.
Her mother began to descend the rocks, below
the bridge, in order to get down to the bed of the
brook, intending to follow it along to the pond.
Lucy wanted to go with her mother, and she also
wanted to see Robert take care of the horse.

" Mother, wait for me," said Lucy.

" I'll go along slowly," said her mother.

" But, mother," said Lucy, " I can't get along,
unless you help me."

" Yes," said her mother, " I think you can.
At any rate, if I find any place where I think
you can't get along, I will wait for you."

Robert went on unharnessing his horse. He
put the several parts of the harness in the wagon
as he took them off, and at last nothing remained
but the bridle.

" Robert," said Lucy, " are you going to fasten
him to a tree ? "

" No," said Robert; " he couldn't eat the
grass, if I should."

" What are you going to do, then ? " said Lucy.

" I am going to let him go where he likes "

"O Robert," said Lucy, "then he'll run away."

"No," said Robert.

Robert then unfastened the throat-lash, and took hold of the bridle, at the top of the horse's head, and drew it over his ears, and off before; and then the bits dropped easily out of his mouth, and the horse, understanding that he was liberated, drew his head away. He walked off a few steps, and then lay down to roll, while Lucy stood laughing heartily at the awkward figure he made, with all his four *heels*, as she called them, in the air.

"*I* believe he'll run away," said Lucy.

"No," said Robert; "he won't run away."

"And, besides, I don't believe you can catch him, and put his bridle on again."

"Yes," said Robert; "I've got some salt in my pocket, on purpose."

Lucy had heard of catching birds by sprinkling salt on their tails, and she stood bewildered and perplexed, trying to imagine how this method was to be applied to Hero, when she heard her mother calling her. So she turned away from Robert, and began to descend the bank, towards her mother, calling out, —

"Yes, mother; I'm coming."

Robert carried the bridle to the wagon, and put it in; and then he pushed the wagon entirely out of the road, so that, if a team were to come by, it would not run against it. After doing that, he followed Lucy and her mother down the bank of the stream.

CHAPTER XIII.

THE RETURN.

THEY found a very pleasant place, indeed, for their luncheon, under some shelving rocks, at the angle between the ravine of the brook and the shore of the pond. They could see the whole surface of the pond, and the woods and mountains beyond. There was only one house in sight, and that was Mr. Emery's. The unfinished end was turned towards them. Lucy took out a mug from the tin pail, and went to the brook to dip up some water, to see if it was cool. Her mother told her, before she went, that she had no doubt it was cool. Lucy found it as her mother had said. It was very cool indeed. She dipped up her mug full from a little, deep place among some stones covered with green moss. It looked very cool, and it proved to be so on tasting it.

Lucy brought a mug of it to her mother.

" Mother," said Lucy, " how did you know it was cool ? "

" Because," said her mother, " brooks become warm when they flow for a long distance across an open country exposed to the rays of the sun. But this brook comes directly down from the mountains, flowing through the woods all the way ; so that I think the water could not have had time to get warm "

" Where does it come from, at first ? " said
Lucy.

" It comes from a spring," said her mother, " I
suppose. Some springs break out of the ground
from under a rock."

" What makes the spring ? " asked Lucy.

" Why, the water in the mountains above," replied her mother, " presses down in among the
rocks, and wherever there is a crevice in the rock
near the surface of the ground, the water comes
out."

" But what makes there be water in the mountains above ? " asked Lucy.

" It comes from rains."

" Then I should think that, when it had done
raining, it would pretty soon stop coming out in'
the spring."

" No," said her mother ; " it takes a great while
to drain off. The earth, and the moss, and the
roots, and the stones, hold the water like a great
sponge. It slowly soaks down, and gets into the
crevices and fissures, and so runs out in a steady
stream, wherever a fissure or any opening of the
rock comes out to the surface. Still, if it has not
rained for a very long while, the springs begin to
grow low, and some of them stop running
entirely."

They staid at this place more than an hour.
After they had eaten their luncheon, they rambled
about among the rocks, and along the shore,
gathering flowers. Lucy amused herself in pick-
ing up pebbles and throwing them into the water.

Robert pointed to a patch of green leaves which were floating upon the water at some distance from the shore, and said that that was a field of lily pads.

"Lily pads," repeated Lucy; "what are lily pads?"

"Why, that is where the pond lilies grow," said Robert. "We come out here sometimes, and get them."

"I never saw any pond lilies," said Lucy. "Are they pretty?"

"O, yes," said Robert, "beautiful. They are white, and just like a star; and when they are open, they are as big as the palm of my hand."

"I wish I could get one," said Lucy.

"I would go and get you one," said Robert, "if it was the right season. But it is too late; they are all gone now."

"How could you get them," asked Lucy's mother, "if there *were* any now?"

"O, we've got a raft," said Robert, "along the shore here a little way. The boys made a raft, and we come and go out on that."

"Boys!" said Lucy's mother with surprise. "I shouldn't think that there would ever be any boys here."

"O, yes," said Robert, "there are a great many boys live about here."

"Why, where?" said Lucy's mother. "Excepting Mr. Emery's house, I have not seen any signs of inhabitants at all. It is all desolation."

There were, however, a great number of farms

15

lying on the various by-roads around, and Lucy's
mother did not know from how wide a circle boys
would gather to get lilies from a pond.

Lucy asked her mother to let her walk along
the shore with Robert, and see his raft.

" How far is it, Robert ? " asked her mother.

" Only a few steps," replied Robert. " But,
then," continued he, " if you would rather not
have her go away, I can bring it along here."

" How ? " said her mother.

" O, I can push it right along," said Robert.

" Well," replied Lucy's mother, " that will be
the best plan."

So Robert went off after his raft, around a
point of land which made out a little way into
the pond, while Lucy continued rambling about
upon the sandy beach, near her mother.

A few minutes afterwards, as Lucy was stooping down to pick up a singular piece of wood,
which had been curiously worn and bleached by
the water, she heard her mother calling to her, —

" Why, Lucy ! look at Robert."

Lucy looked up, and saw Robert just coming
into view, with his raft, around the point of land.

" Why, he's sailing on the raft," said her mother. " I did not know he meant to come in that
way. I thought he was going to push it along
by the shore."

Robert said that he was going to push it, it is
true ; but. he meant, push it by means of a pole,
with himself upon it. Lucy and her mother
were both a little afraid that he might get in ; but,

"'Why, Lucy! look at Robert,' said her mother."— Page 170.

as he seemed entirely at his ease, and uncon-
cerned, they gradually dismissed their fears, and
watched his progress as he slowly approached
them. Lucy was very much interested in the
examination of the raft, as it drew near. It was
made of logs which the boys had cut from the
woods, with smaller pieces laid across and pinned
on, to keep it all together. On the whole, they
concluded that it was a very strong and substantial raft. Robert sailed about upon it for some
time.

Lucy wanted him to go out to the lily pads, to
see if there might not be, possibly, one left ; but
her mother was afraïd to have him go out where
it was so deep. Besides, Robert said that he
was sure that not a single lily could be found, for
it was altogether beyond the season of them.

While Robert was sailing about upon his raft
in the shallow water, Lucy had a long conversation with her mother about springs, brooks, and
ponds. Her mother told her that ponds were
occasioned by there being a natural hollow place
among the mountains, surrounded by high land
on all sides, so that the water which ran into it
from brooks and springs, could not run out until
it rose high enough to run over at the lowest
place in the surrounding land ; and that that was
the outlet. She also explained to her how it
happened that some brooks ran very swiftly,
tumbling over rocks, and others flowed deep and
smooth, and almost still. At length they concluded that it was time to go home. So she took

the pail, and Lucy and her mother went back up the ravine to the road, while Robert sailed back on his raft behind the point of land; for he said that he must put the raft away where it belonged.

Robert did not come back to the mouth of the brook again, but he climbed up the bank into the road, at the place where he fastened the raft. Lucy and her mother sat down upon the end of one of the great logs, on the side of the bridge, and waited for Robert to catch the horse, and harness him. The horse was grazing by the side of the road, at a little distance from the bridge; but not on the side where Robert was coming. Robert therefore had to go across the bridge, to catch him. As he was passing by Lucy and her mother, he put his hand into his pocket, and took out something folded up in a piece of brown paper.

"Is that the salt?" said Lucy.

"Yes," said Robert.

So Robert opened the paper, and began to call out to the horse, —

"Hero! Hero! Hero! Hero!"

Hero paid no attention to the call, but went on quietly cropping the grass.

"Hero! Hero! Hero! Hero!" said Robert, walking along towards him.

Hero lifted up his head, turned it deliberately towards Robert, looked at him a moment, and then put it down again. He took two more mouthfuls of grass, and then turned around, beginning to walk towards Robert.

Robert stopped on the end of the bridge, and waited for him, holding out the paper in his hand. When Hero got near, Robert stooped down, and poured out the salt upon the plank floor of the bridge. To Lucy's surprise, the horse came to the place, and began to lick up the salt with his great tongue. While he was doing it, Robert put the bridle on. Then he stood still, and let the horse finish eating the salt, and then led him away.

"*I* shouldn't like to eat so much salt," said Lucy.

Robert harnessed the horse into the wagon, and then they got in, and drove away. They rode an hour or two by a way which went winding around among forests and mountains, sometimes opening before them, so that they could see wide prospects, and sometimes shut in by rocks, and towering trees, which overhung the road, and made it sombre and solitary.

After a time, they began to ascend a pretty steep and winding road, shut in by the forests and mountains. Sometimes they had by their side, as they travelled slowly along, a noisy brook, sometimes a morass, covered with cedars and firs; and sometimes an impenetrable thicket growing out of steep slopes of land covered with moss, and rocks, and trunks of fallen trees. All this time they were constantly ascending. Still, although they were gradually gaining a high elevation, they had no prospect; for their view was shut in by the forests and mountains all around them. At length, they came to a piece of road which was level. The horse began to trot. It was the first time that he had trotted for nearly half an hour.

" Here is some level road," said Lucy. " I'm glad of it, for now we can go faster."

" Yes," said Robert; " we've got to the height of land."

" What is that ? " said Lucy.

" Why, the highest place. Pretty soon, we shall be going down again."

They came to the end of the level road pretty soon, and then began to descend a little ; and presently, at a turn of the road, they came out to a place where they suddenly had a very extensive and magnificent prospect opened before them.

" O mother," said Lucy, " how far we can see ! "

" Yes," said her mother. " Stop a minute, Robert, and let us look at this prospect.

" Why, Robert," said she again, in a moment, " there is your father's house ! "

She pointed to a house away before them, very far down the valley.

" Yes," said Robert; " we can always see it from here, very plainly. And I can see this rock from our yard."

Robert pointed to a great rocky precipice by the side of the road, and he said that they once came and built a fire upon it, and his mother could see the smoke at their door, very plainly. Lucy was very much surprised to see how low down in the valley the house appeared. They could see the stream beyond it, and Robert pointed out to them the fording-place, where they had crossed on their way, when they first came to the General's. The General's house seemed now to be nearly down upon a level with the water. This was an illusion, occasioned by their high position. They could see the mill-pond, too, and the bridge ; and Lucy showed her mother the green store where she and Comfort went a-shopping. She tried also to see the great stone, where they got caught by the water from the mill ; but it was not to be seen. Lucy thought it was hidden by the mill.

They gazed around upon the prospect for some time, and then Robert began to move on towards home. In fact, it was getting near the evening ; and they saw some clouds in the west, which made them think it was possible that there might be a shower coming.

The road was now generally descending ; so Robert made Hero go pretty fast. The clouds behind them, however, increased. At last, one, blacker and larger than the rest, appeared to be coming up, and Lucy's mother said that she believed that there was going to be a shower. But she was mistaken. It rose higher and higher, and for a time appeared threatening ; but, after all, it brought nothing with it but a gust of wind. After this had passed, the sky was somewhat clearer, though the sun had set, and the twilight was fast coming on. Lucy suddenly discovered a very bright star in the middle of a large open place among the clouds ; and she exclaimed, —

" O mother, see that star ! "

" Yes," said her mother; " that's Venus, I really believe.   Yes, it must be Venus."

" The evening star ? " said Lucy.

" Yes," said her mother ; " see how bright it is ; and yet you cannot see any other star in the sky."

Lucy looked all around, but no other star was to be seen.   The sky was somewhat obscured by clouds ; but in the spaces between the clouds there were no stars to be seen.

" You see, Lucy," said her mother, " that it would not have done any good for you to have got up early to see the morning star ; for Venus is the evening star now ; the sun is before her."

" Yes, mother," said Lucy.

" And so, being before her," continued her mother, " the sun goes down, and leaves Venus a little way up in the sky.   Of course, when he rises in the morning, he leaves Venus a little below the horizon, where she is out of sight."

" How fast Venus goes ! " said Lucy.

" No," said her mother ; " it is the motion of the clouds which makes it look as if Venus was going fast.   But yet she is going down slowly. If you notice how high she is now, and then again when we get home, you will see that she has gone down considerably."

Lucy said that she meant to watch Venus. But she did not watch her very long, for her attention was attracted by a large light, some dis-

tance before them. It was in the direction of the
General's house. Lucy and her mother both saw
it at the same time. Lucy thought it was a beautiful light, but her mother was frightened. She
was afraid that it was the General's house on fire.

" No," said Robert; " it is not our house. It
is this side of our house. It must be some fire in
the woods."

" But who should be building fires in the
woods this time of the day ? " asked her mother.

" I don't know," replied Robert ; " only I know
that there often are fires about."

As they went on, the light grew broader and
brighter. Presently they thought they saw the
flash of a flame, and then some sparks ascending.

" What can it be ? " said Robert. " It looks
as if it was near my clearing. There ! " he exclaimed again, after a moment's pause, " I know
what it is. It is that great heap which we tried
to set on fire."

" That heap ? " said Lucy

" Yes," said Robert; " I've no doubt it's that
heap. The fire has been working under it all
day, heating it through, and now these gusts of
wind have set it a-going."

Robert was right. Lucy's mother could hardly
believe that fire could have remained inactive
under such a heap of combustibles, and finally
break out, after so long an interval. But it was
really so. The wood which they had put under
it, had set some of the lower parts of the heap on
fire, and they had burned away slowly ; while the

hot air and gases, rising up through the heap, had been gradually drying it; and now the wind had fanned the whole up into a flame. The light of the fire grew brighter and brighter as they drew nearer, although they could not get a distinct view of it, on account of trees which intervened. At length, however, when they reached the part of the road which was opposite to it, the whole burst at once upon their view, blazing, crackling, and roaring, in a manner almost terrific. Lucy's mother said it was quite a conflagration. The whole heap was a burning mass from top to bottom. The forms of all the crooked logs and stumps were yet preserved, but they were all of the brightest red; and the flames curled and flashed above in the most furious manner. If Hero had not been an uncommonly docile horse, he would have fled in terror. A vast column, of smoke and sparks ascended from the heap, far up into the dark sky.

They looked at it a few minutes, and then drove home. When they got out of the wagon, and were going into the house, they stopped a moment on the door-step, to look back at Venus and the fire. Venus was just going down, and the bright glow of the fire was very distinctly visible behind a hill.

THE END.